PENGUIN BOOKS

ANDAMAN ADVENTURE: THE JARAWA

Deepak Dalal gave up a career in chemical engineering to write stories for children. He lives in Pune with his wife, two daughters and several dogs and cats. He enjoys wildlife, nature and the outdoors. His books include the Vikram–Aditya adventure series (for older readers) and the Feather Tales series (for younger readers). All his stories have a strong conservation theme.

A
VIKRAM–ADITYA
STORY

ANDAMAN ADVENTURE

THE JARAWA

DEEPAK DALAL

PENGUIN BOOKS
An imprint of Penguin Random House

PENGUIN BOOKS

USA | Canada | UK | Ireland | Australia
New Zealand | India | South Africa | China

Penguin Books is part of the Penguin Random House group of companies
whose addresses can be found at global.penguinrandomhouse.com

Published by Penguin Random House India Pvt. Ltd
4th Floor, Capital Tower 1, MG Road,
Gurugram 122 002, Haryana, India

First published by Tarini Publishing 2000
Andaman Adventure: The Jarawa was published by Silverfish, an imprint of Grey
Oak Publishers, in association with Westland Publications Private Limited 2013
This edition published in Penguin Books by Penguin Random House India 2022

Inside illustrations: Anusha Menon and Samar Bansal

10 9 8 7 6 5 4 3 2 1

ISBN 9780143449409

Layout design: Samar Bansal
Typeset in Adobe Caslon Pro by Manipal Technologies Limited, Manipal
Printed at Replika Press Pvt. Ltd, India

www.penguin.co.in

For the late Dr Ravi Sankaran–an outstanding field researcher and friend

THE ANDAMAN ISLANDS

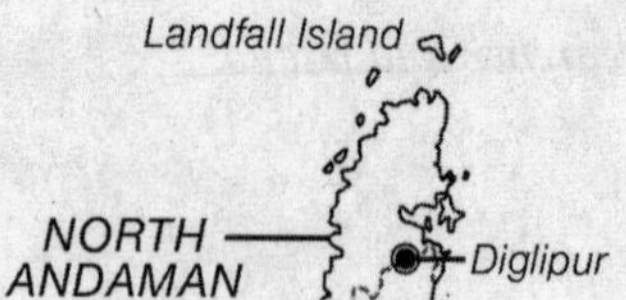

OF BIRDS, NATIVES AND ISLANDS

Dear Vikram,

My friend, Dr Ravi Shankaran, is as elusive as a snow leopard. You would think that contacting someone these days is just a matter of picking up the phone or sending an e-mail. But Ravi Shankaran and the Andaman Islands have proved that it is not so. Though it can be frustrating, I actually find it reassuring that there are still places on this planet where you can disappear and remain untraceable. I had to work harder for sure, but I finally tracked my old friend down.

Time for the good news now. Dr Shankaran has agreed to be your host in the islands. I can finally confirm your winter holiday destination. Aditya's too—I have spoken to his father, and he has consented. Yes, both of you are off to the Andaman Islands!

The news will delight you, I'm sure. You love islands. The great joy of your stay in the Lakshadweep Islands is still fresh in my mind. The Andaman Islands, however, are very different from the tiny coral atolls of Lakshadweep. In the vast seas of our world the Lakshadweep Islands are mere pebbles, whereas the Andamans are big like boulders, in comparison.

The largest and most important islands in the Andaman group are the South, Middle and North Andaman Islands (I've attached a map for you, have a look). They constitute the main body of the Andman group. They lie close to one another and are separated by narrow straits. Today, a 200-kilometre road, called the Andaman Trunk Road, connects the three islands—all the way from Port Blair in the south, to a city called Diglipur in the north.

The other large island is 'Little Andaman', located south of the main group. Then you have mid-sized islands like Havelock and Interview. Havelock is a popular tourist destination with wonderful beaches, whereas Interview (odd name, isn't it?) is a forest sanctuary where no one lives.

Like every archipelago, the Andaman chain possesses hundreds of small islands. Some are mere specks with quaint names like North Button, Middle Button, South Button, and there is even one called Guitar Island. No one lives on these little islands except for birds and animals, and turtles that visit.

Not many people know that India's only active volcano lies in the Andaman Islands. Far out in the Andaman Sea, on the eastern extremity of the archipelago, lie two islands called Barren and Narcondum. The volcano on Narcondum is long dead but the one on Barren isn't. It last erupted just a few years ago and people say that it might do so again.

The Andamans are an island paradise. There are several such bewitching island chains scattered about the seas of our world, but the Andamans possess something unique—something no other archipelago can match. When you fly into Port Blair, your aircraft will pass over an island called North Sentinel. From the air, North Sentinel could be any other island. You will see a beach, forests, and a fringing coral reef. But hidden beneath that forest is one of our planet's last human treasures. North Sentinel Island is the home of a race of people, the like of which you will find nowhere else on earth.

This tiny tribe—called the Sentinelese—are a people forgotten by time. Their entire universe is limited to the boundaries of their little island. Can you imagine that none of them have ever crossed that boundary and that they have no idea what lies beyond the waters surrounding their island home? Sounds ridiculous, doesn't it? We live in a world of space travel and instant communication—yet, we have humans who haven't progressed beyond the Stone Age! 'Nonsense!' is what most people would say. But islands, especially isolated ones like the Andamans, are curious places where, through quirks of geography and history, strange happenings are commonplace.

The Sentinelese are a dark-skinned people. They hunt with bows and arrows, and they wear no clothes. There are those who will call such people 'primitive' or dub them 'savages', but not I. The Sentinelese are a unique people on our earth—a national, or, I daresay, an international treasure. People like them do not exist anymore. Everybody on earth has been touched by what we call civilisation and progress.

But not the Sentinelese. Unblemished by civilisation, they live a life that has remained unchanged over millennia.

The entire Andaman Archipelago was once the home of a black race. The islands belonged exclusively to them for thousands of years. Secluded from the rest of the world, they prospered and evolved into several distinct tribes. Then in 1858, the British decided to set up a penal colony on the islands. That decision proved calamitous for the natives. In the years since, almost all the tribes that once roamed the Andamans have been wiped out. Today, only the Sentinelese, and two other tribes, called the Jarawa and the Onge, survive. The Great Andamanese (once the largest tribe) now number no more than forty individuals, and, like several endangered animal species on our earth, they will soon cease to exist.

The Sentinelese have been lucky. Their island of North Sentinel lies some distance from the main group, so no one goes there. Those who have tried have been showered with arrows and spears. A combination of geography and hostility has allowed them to survive more or less untouched. The Onge are a tribe that live on Little Andaman Island. They too have survived but because of close contact with settlers that live on Little Andaman, they are abandoning their forest ways.

There is one tribe, however, that refuses to give up its forest ways. These people are called the Jarawa. The durability of the Jarawa is remarkable because they reside in the heart of the main group of islands. Unlike the Sentinelese who are isolated on their island, the Jarawa are surrounded by settlers and farmers. The Andaman Trunk

Road passes through their land. The Jarawa are aware of us and the lives we lead, yet they shun civilisation and prefer their own ways.

I have been lucky to have come across them once, and it is a sight I will never forget. Dr Shankaran and I were returning from Interview Island by boat. We were sailing down the Jarawa coast, heading for Port Blair. The sun was setting when we spotted a group of Jarawa on one of the beaches. They had seen us too and were dancing. There were men, women and children. None of them wore clothes and we could see that they were lean and healthy. Though they possessed bows and arrows they weren't in any way hostile to us. They were dancing out of sheer exuberance, and I think they were happy to see us. It was a wonderful moment. I couldn't believe that I was face-to-face with such an ancient people. We were all human beings, yet so different from each other. Their way of life was pure and their needs so simple that the forest provided them all they wanted. Whereas we are slaves to modern civilisation, always craving more than our planet can provide.

The Jarawa might be simple in their ways, but they are a proud people. There are those who have tried to take advantage of them, and, to their discomfiture, have discovered that the Jarawa are fierce when troubled and do not take kindly to being meddled with. The Andaman administration has banned entry into the Jarawa Reserve, more for our safety than theirs. My encounter with them was fortuitous and peaceable. You and Aditya will be sailing along their coast too, and I hope that Lady Luck will smile on you, like she did on me.

A word about my friend, Dr Shankaran, and his work. Dr Shankaran is an ornithologist. He has taken residence on the islands to ensure the survival of a tiny bird called the 'edible nest swiftlet'. These small, black birds are unique in a rather surprising manner. As you know, birds construct their nests from twigs, bark, branches, mud, rope and whatever else they can find. The edible nest swiftlet, however, does not collect material to build its nest. Rather, it secretes its entire nest. Equipped with extraordinary salivary glands, it secretes pale, half-moon shaped nests. Because the nest has been entirely secreted by the bird, it is edible—hence the name 'edible' nest swiftlet. Now, if the nests weren't edible, there wouldn't be a problem. But humans have a taste for anything edible, and that has proved disastrous for these tiny birds. You might have heard of 'Bird's Nest Soup'—it is a delicacy served in restaurants across the Far Eastern countries, such as China, Taiwan and Singapore. This expensive soup is stewed from powdered fragments of the swiftlet's nest. The milky-white material of the nest is reputed to have outstanding medicinal properties and is also used as a key ingredient in various traditional medicines in those countries. Because of these 'supposed' properties, the nests are much sought after. People have been destroying nesting colonies of the swiftlets for years to collect the nests, and consequently the population of these birds has dwindled significantly.

The swiftlets nest in caves all over the Andaman Islands. Today, almost every nesting cave in the islands is under siege from poachers, and it isn't surprising that the birds are critically endangered.

Dr Shankaran hopes to turn things around. The first step he has taken is to protect the caves. It isn't physically possible for him to police every cave on the islands, so he has chosen a few that lie in ecologically sensitive areas.

Interview Island, as I mentioned earlier, is a sanctuary. There are several swiftlet caves on the island. Selecting them for protection, Dr Shankaran has pitched camp on Interview beside the caves. His efforts, I am delighted to say, have already borne fruit. Because of the watchful presence of his guards, a batch of chicks has hatched safely, without having their nests stolen. This was the first successful nesting from those caves in years, and it was a momentous occasion when some thousand young birds took wing from them.

You and Aditya are in luck. Dr Shankaran has specially arranged a trip to his camp at Interview. The island, besides its swiftlet caves, possesses magnificent forests and fabulous beaches. His offer is a rare opportunity, and I hope you will make the best of it.

Dr Shankaran will not be with you for the first week of your stay in the islands, but he has made arrangements for his daughter, Chitra, to look after you. I last met Chitra years ago when she was just a toddler. She was a handful even then. I recollect that her favourite pastime was catching snakes and snaring lizards. Her father tells me that she hasn't changed much except that she is six feet tall now and that her passion for reptiles also includes crocodiles. She finished school last year and has taken a break from her studies to be with her father in the Andaman Islands. Her father, poor fellow, has had a hard time looking after her. She is quite unstoppable, he says. During the six months she has been there, she has travelled the length and breadth of the islands and almost everybody in the Andamans knows of her. She has earned a diving certificate too. I have told Dr Shankaran about your love for the undersea world, and he says arranging dives won't be a problem—Chitra will do what is required. The girl has a forceful personality, I'm told, and I have been asked to warn both of you accordingly. I personally don't perceive a problem considering that you all share a deep love for the outdoors and nature. I am sure Chitra will look after you well and that all of you will have a wonderful time.

I have forgotten to touch upon the history of the islands in this rather long letter. Maybe it is best that way because at Port Blair you simply cannot escape history. The Andaman Islands are inextricably linked to our freedom struggle.

I am sure they have taught you about 'Kalapani' at school. History will come alive for you at the Cellular Jail at Port Blair. Have a good time discovering it all. Stay in touch, Vikram. Don't go underground like Dr Shankaran, and call me often.

Affectionately,
Your loving father

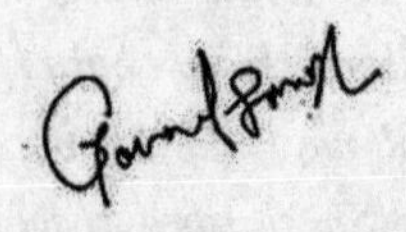

PS: Don't forget to fortify yourselves against malaria before leaving Port Blair. Though not rampant, the disease does strike the odd visitor. Ask Chitra, she'll get you the tablets.

THE JARAWA COAST

'It's against the law to camp on Jarawa land,' said Vikram, for possibly the tenth time.

Chitra glared at him. 'Why don't you pay attention to what I'm saying? We are not camping on Jarawa land. We are only going to park our boat on one of their beaches.'

'That's exactly what's not allowed.'

Aditya, who was sitting beside Vikram, butted in. 'Parking a boat is not the same as setting up camp.'

Vikram breathed deeply, staring sightlessly at the blue expanse surrounding him, wishing he had never left Port Blair. Though it was only three days since their expedition had begun, he had lost count of the arguments that had raged on board.

He tried to be reasonable once more. 'It *is* the same. We will be trespassing whether we park or camp on their land.'

Chitra's response was immediate. 'That's not true! To trespass means to enter, to walk on their land. We're only parking a boat and leaving. Don't you get it—leaving!'

'Leaving for where, Chitra? It's where you intend to go that is far more illegal than parking a boat on a Jarawa beach.'

Chitra's tone turned shriller as it normally did when disputes warmed up. 'How can that be? We won't be setting foot on their reserve after that. We'll be travelling in a creek on a dinghy.'

'The creek you intend to travel on is a Jarawa creek. The creek winds deep into their territory, into areas we are forbidden from going.'

Chitra's tone climbed a few notches. 'We will be entering at night. If it is the Jarawa you are worried about, let me assure you that they do not move about at night. And they do not camp near creeks. They are afraid of crocodiles, and sandflies would trouble them.'

'Come on, Vikram.' It was Aditya now. 'We're going in there to see crocodiles. We're going to have fun. It's going to be an adventure. These aren't ordinary crocs we're talking about. They are saltwater crocodiles—the largest crocs in India. How can you miss out on such a fabulous opportunity? We'll be entering under cover of darkness and only for a couple of hours. No one will know.'

Vikram refused to be persuaded. 'Why do we have to choose a Jarawa creek? There are creeks all along the Andaman coastline. We can find crocs down any of them without breaking the law.'

'Because Jarawa creeks swarm with crocodiles,' said Chitra. 'Other creeks are not protected, and crocodiles are poached in their waters. This creek is not just a crocodile haven. You will be entering a sanctuary. It is an incomparable wilderness.'

Vikram hesitated but recovered fast. 'Stop trying to tempt me, Chitra. Of course, I want to search for crocodiles. I know what I will be missing. But what if things go wrong? None of us have travelled down that creek. It will be dark. We don't know what to expect. What if we hit logs in the water, take a wrong turn, or run aground? I don't want to be stranded in Jarawa territory.'

Chitra pointed to the rear of the boat. A short, muscular man with Burmese features was sitting bare-chested beside the engine, his hand on the rudder. 'Let's settle this argument,' she said firmly. 'Alex, our boatman, is a neutral party. He will be at the controls if we travel down the creek. He knows how far to go and what's dangerous. He is a cautious man and is also mortally afraid of the Jarawa. Let's leave the decision to him. Aditya and I will abide by whatever he says. Right, Aditya?'

'Sounds fair to me.'

Chitra rounded on Vikram. 'That's two of us. How about you?'

Though Chitra's offer sounded reasonable, Vikram wasn't sure it was. Alex worshipped Chitra, and though technically he was in charge of their expedition, he rarely opposed Chitra's directives and commands. But to give Chitra credit, it was true that Alex was terrified of the Jarawa. Also, as Vikram had witnessed the past few days, the man was conservative by nature. It was possible that his decision would be balanced and fair.

'Okay,' sighed Vikram. 'I accept.'

The sun was nudging a distant bank of clouds, low on the western horizon, as Chitra threaded her way to the aft section of the boat. The shimmering waters of the Bay of Bengal stretched as far as the eye could see to their left. But it wasn't the sea that drew Vikram's gaze. He had hardly glanced at its blue expanse since the Jarawa coast had appeared, and even now, he turned his eyes to the shore that was slipping past a few hundred metres to their right. It was a rugged coastline, mostly rocky—beaches had been rare. The forest, however, had been a constant. An endless band of trees lined the Jarawa coast. The trees were tall and densely packed, standing like an impenetrable wall, as if shielding the island's dwellers from prying eyes. Vikram had gazed at the coast as it unfurled its green fortifications, hoping for a repeat of his father's experience. But the Jarawa, if they were there, had refused to oblige.

The boat they were travelling on was long and narrow, a 'dugout', hewed from a single tree trunk. Common in the Andaman Islands, dugout boats were known locally as 'dungis'. Vikram turned to the aft section of the dungi. Chitra was seated there beside Alex, towering almost a foot above him. Behind them, bobbing in the water, was a grey Gemini rubber dinghy, fitted with an outboard motor. Rather than stowing it on board, they were towing it along behind them.

Alex was sitting silently, listening to Chitra who appeared to have a lot to say. He should have known better, thought Vikram, as he watched the girl speak forcefully to the boatman. Influencing Alex was not part of the deal she had struck with him. It was uncanny how

Chitra adopted the same crooked tactics as his school-friend, Aditya. Together, his companions were a handful, and Vikram, having survived three days in their company, seriously began to wonder how he would cope for the rest of their holiday.

The similarity between Chitra and Aditya was not restricted to their personalities. They were comparable physically too. Both were six feet tall and blessed with handsome features. Aditya, with his shaggy mop of hair, was good-looking in a dashing, male sort of way; while Chitra, though she spurned make-up and most feminine accessories, possessed attractive, strong-boned features.

Chitra and Aditya had hit it off at the very start of their journey. Vikram hadn't anticipated their bonding. Given their strong-willed temperaments he had expected fireworks and clashes. But a healthy rivalry had taken charge instead. Whether it was swimming in the sea, or riding motorcycles in Port Blair, or setting up camp on a deserted island, or diving deep to search for fish and coral—they continuously strived to outdo each other, revelling in the competition.

Alex had handed the rudder to Chitra and was crossing to where Vikram and Aditya sat.

Aditya grinned. 'What bet you're going to lose?'

'You mean Chitra has bullied him into saying yes?'

'That's your take, not mine. Wasn't it you who taught me that all is fair in love and war?'

Alex was of Burmese descent. He was a Karen Burmese. Many Karen families had been brought to the Andaman Islands from Myanmar by the British, during their rule. Though the British had since departed, the Karens had stayed on and were Indian citizens now. Karens were traditionally good sailors, and Alex was one of Dr Shankaran's trusted employees.

Vikram spoke after Alex had settled himself. 'You heard what Chitra wants to do.'

'Yes. Chitra madam tell me.' For a strong, burly man Alex's voice was surprisingly soft.

'What about the Jarawa? You know there could be trouble.'

Alex nodded gravely. 'Yes. They no like us Burmese. They kill if they see us. Two my friends . . . killed by Jarawa.'

'Is it safe then to park our boat on their land and motor up one of their creeks?'

Alex dropped his gaze, taking a sudden interest in the planks at his feet. 'When we fill fuel at Uttara jetty I ask about Jarawa there,' he said, not looking up. 'People say they all south at Spike Island and Lakda Lungta—no Jarawa here at Lewis Inlet.'

'How can you be sure?' asked Vikram.

'Jarawa always moving. They stay in one place two weeks . . . one month, then move on. All gone south. Lewis Inlet okay. Parking boat on beach no problem. I been down the creek with Dr Shankaran. No meet Jarawa, only crocodiles. Plenty crocodiles. Creek is safe, no problem.'

Aditya was smirking in the background.

Vikram fumed. The Karen was hiding his fear. He was sure of it. Chitra had prevailed over Alex's common sense, and Vikram did not like it. The girl had outmanoeuvred him.

Vikram turned to Aditya as Alex trudged back to the boat controls. 'You and Chitra plotted this, didn't you? I should have guessed when you delayed our morning start. I had wanted to leave early so we could reach Interview by nightfall, but both of you delayed it, blaming the rain and the weather. Now I understand why you dawdled! It was to make sure we reached Lewis Inlet by sundown instead; so that we'd be forced to camp there, and you'd be able to sneak a visit to the creek at night.'

Aditya smiled broadly. 'Loosen up, Vikram. Forget the morning. It's in the past. Think about the evening instead. The creek is a pristine wilderness—Chitra says so. We'll be spotting crocs in the dark. It's going to be an evening you won't forget!'

Vikram did eventually loosen up, but he took his time. He sat apart from Chitra and Aditya as the boat droned on up the forested coast. The sea was bright and blue, yet he preferred the forest, staring intently at it as it slipped endlessly by.

Alex disturbed him sometime later with a loud call. Along with Chitra and Aditya, Vikram rushed to the rear of the boat where Alex was hauling in a line of blue nylon that trailed in the water. They crowded around the sturdy Karen as he pulled in a long, silvery fish from the sea.

'Your dinner,' grinned Alex, as he despatched the unfortunate creature and stuffed it in a cloth bag.

Alex yelled a similar call another half-hour later. He was turning the dungi shoreward and Vikram spotted a tiny beach nestling in the forest.

'Lewis Inlet,' shouted Chitra, pointing.

A column of rocks protruded into the sea some distance ahead. There was a gap in the coast after the rocks. The gap was broad, and the shore resumed where it ended.

'We're going in now,' cried Chitra. 'We'll park our boat on the beach, unload our camping gear and cook dinner. The sun will be setting soon, and it should be dark by the time we finish our meal. We'll pack up and leave for the creek immediately after.'

The sea was calm, and the sky was turning red as Alex smoothly guided the boat in. When he cut the engine the only sound was that of waves and the cry of birds. The forest stood tall and shadowy behind the beach. Despite himself, Vikram felt a thrill pulse through him. He was about to set foot on Jarawa territory. He jumped into the water along with his friends and together they helped Alex secure the dungi.

'Aditya, you and Vikram unload the rucksacks,' instructed Chitra. 'I'll help Alex with the cooking equipment.'

Utensils and camping gear were hauled across the water and stacked on the beach. Alex then requested them to collect dry wood, which the three teenagers quickly set about, casting nervous glances into the forest. But no arrows flew from the foliage and no Jarawa materialised from the trees. All they heard was the buzz of crickets and the calls of bashful, hidden birds.

Aditya lit and stoked a fire while Chitra and Vikram helped Alex prepare a meal of fish curry and rice. Soon the fire was hissing, and their meal was simmering in two vessels balanced securely above the flames.

Chitra stretched her long legs on the sand. 'See, Vikram. Didn't I tell you—no Jarawa here. You were making a fuss about nothing.'

Aditya defended his friend. 'Vikram is naturally cautious. In any case, he's over it now, right Vikram?'

But Vikram did not reply. Turning, Aditya saw he was gazing out to sea. Alex was also staring across the darkening waters. At first Aditya did not spot what had attracted their attention, but when he shielded his eyes from the setting sun, he saw it too. A flicker of green was visible on the crimson sea.

'We've got company,' said Chitra, shading her eyes. 'Any idea who it could be, Alex?'

Alex did not reply. His face was turning a purplish shade of red and as the boat drew nearer, he swore unintelligibly in Burmese.

Vikram reached for his rucksack and dug out a pair of binoculars. 'It's a dungi,' he confirmed, gazing through them. 'Odd colour though . . . bright green. There are four men on board, and it's headed our way.'

'Are they in uniform?' Chitra spoke nervously.

'No, they don't seem to be. Some have Burmese faces, like Alex.'

Chitra breathed a sigh of relief. 'That's okay then. There shouldn't be any trouble.'

Aditya looked at Chitra. 'Why? Were you expecting any?'

Vikram lowered his binoculars. 'Have you forgotten that we've broken the law, Aditya? We're not supposed to be camped here. If the boat belonged to the navy or the coastguard, we would have been in trouble. Ask Chitra.'

'There could have been a problem,' admitted Chitra.

'Burmese faces are all right, though. They are probably Karens like Alex, out on a fishing trip. Hey, what's wrong with Alex, just look at him.'

All the while they had known Alex neither Vikram nor Aditya had seen him display emotion. The Karen smiled when spoken to but otherwise his expression was blank, like a cloudless sky. Now, however, his expression was distinctly stormy, and he was waving a fist and muttering.

'What's up, Alex?' enquired Chitra. 'Anything bothering you?'

'That man on boat is bad man, big danger.' Alex shook as he spoke.

'You know him?'

'My cousin!' Alex spat the words out.

Chitra frowned. 'Then why are you angry? You should be glad to see him.'

But Alex did not answer. Instead, he strode across the sand and waded into the sea.

'Grab your seats, everybody!' announced Aditya. 'We have a Karen family feud for the evening's entertainment.'

'Showdown at Jarawa Creek,' quipped Vikram.

Chitra whistled as she stared at the approaching green vessel. 'Wow . . . I've never seen Alex so angry before.' She spoke thoughtfully. 'I wonder who this man is. I know Alex's family well. I've stayed often at his house, and I've met his relatives. They're all on good terms as far as I know.'

The flaming disc of the sun sank into the sea as the dungi cut its engine and drew up beside theirs. Vikram experienced a stinging sensation on his arms and legs but ignored it as he watched. A man leapt out of the dungi and waded towards Alex. He was tall and well built. Like Alex, all he wore was a pair of shorts. Vikram spotted some kind of a pattern, like a tattoo, a big one, on his chest.

'Darned mosquitoes!' growled Aditya, smacking his legs.

Chitra slapped her wrists. 'Oh no! Sandflies! This beach has sandflies!'

A heated exchange had started on the water. The tall man and Alex were shouting at one another. A second man had jumped out of the dungi and was holding the boat steady as it bobbed on the waves. The other two sat on board, watching keenly. The altercation was conducted entirely in Burmese.

Vikram spanked his arms and legs. He felt as if he were being stung by a swarm of bees. They had camped twice earlier on deserted beaches but only mosquitoes had bothered them. Though troublesome, the mosquito offensive was like gentle prods compared to the sandfly assault.

The noise level of the dispute was climbing, but Aditya had more compelling matters on his mind. 'The mosquito repellent!' he cried. 'Who's got the tube?'

Chitra stroked her arms. 'The ointment's not going to help. Nothing stops sandflies. You'll have to endure them, Aditya. But don't worry, they aren't active for long. They'll be gone in minutes.'

The squabble was getting more and more heated. Vikram was beginning to wonder whether it would deteriorate into a brawl when it suddenly ended. The tall man abruptly returned to his dungi. Alex turned too and trooped back to the shore, his expression murderous.

'Who he think he is?' snarled Alex, as he flung himself on to the sand beside the fire. 'Is he policeman . . . how dare he tell me to leave? I won't go.'

Chitra cleared her throat. 'He . . . uh, asked us to leave?' she asked delicately.

This launched a fresh tirade from Alex. He leapt back to his feet and ranted in Burmese, shaking a fist at the departing dungi. Chitra sensibly refrained from asking any further questions.

The prancing flame of the fire turned brighter as the sky darkened. A brilliant moon, not quite full yet, shone from a cloudless sky. A flock of egrets winged silently above the water, flashing silver in the moonlight.

Dinner was ready soon. They tucked into the simple meal, enjoying it thoroughly. Alex recovered his composure as he ate. When the meal was finished, Chitra enquired about the altercation once again.

'Patrick is my cousin,' said Alex, licking his fingers. 'We grow up together. We same age, but never friends. Patrick is a bad man. He kill my best friend. I know he did but police afraid of him. Never catch him.'

Chitra stared, open-mouthed. 'A murderer?'

Alex nodded grimly.

After an awkward pause Vikram broke the silence. 'You said he asked us to leave.'

Alex's face clouded again. 'He is not policeman. Why I listen to him? He wants us go away. Camping not allowed here, he say. I tell him mind his business.'

'But why would he ask us to leave?' repeated Vikram.

'He is doing bad business,' said Alex. 'Why else? He is smuggler, poacher. He do wrong things here and not want us to see. But I no care. We will go for crocodiles. He can't stop us. Come, we leave, it is late.'

The dishes and utensils were washed in seawater. Alex waded out to rope in the dinghy and the teenagers excitedly prepared themselves for the expedition.

'Take your windcheaters along,' instructed Chitra. 'It will get cold as the night progresses. Carry your torches too.'

Vikram retrieved his windcheater from his rucksack and slipped it on.

'That's useful gear,' he said approvingly, as Chitra buckled a thick belt over her windcheater. The belt had a pouch in front and compartments on either side in which water bottles were strapped.

Chitra grinned as she fastened her straps. 'I use it all the time. There's a torch, penknife and compass inside the pouch. It's useful for food and water too. I've packed biscuits and our morning chapatis inside. It's always nice to have a bite handy.'

'I second that,' declared Aditya, zipping his jacket. 'Come on, Alex is waiting.'

But Chitra halted him. 'We have to douse the fire first. Get water from the sea. We need to dampen the logs to ensure they don't kindle again.'

Vikram and Aditya collected a cooking vessel each and started for the sea. But Aditya had barely taken a couple of steps when he suddenly yelled. The vessel flew from his hand as he flung himself sideways, landing heavily on the sand. Vikram saw what had upended Aditya, and he too backed hurriedly away.

'*Snake*,' stuttered Aditya. 'There's a snake on the sand.'

Chitra's response was exactly the reverse of the boys. Instead of backing away she hurried forward.

The snake was a wrinkle in the sand. It wasn't long, barely a metre in length. Moonlight revealed a set of tightly coiled bands on its body and there was something odd about its tail. While the rest of its body was typically round, its tail was flattened, like a paddle.

'That's a sea snake, boys,' said Chitra, halting beside it.

Vikram spoke in a strained voice. 'Shouldn't you back off? Aren't sea snakes the most venomous snakes in the world?'

Aditya crawled further away on hearing this.

'What are you doing?' cried Vikram. Chitra had dropped to a crouch beside the snake, her feet just a short distance from its banded coils.

'Are you insane?' barked Aditya. 'Do you want to die?'

'Take it easy, Aditya,' calmed Chitra. 'Has no one taught you about snakes? They are scared of us. They don't attack unless in self-defence. I'm not threatening the snake; it doesn't mind my presence. Stop cowering, and come and stand beside me. Nothing's going to happen.'

Vikram saw Aditya stiffen in the firelight. His inelegant dive had embarrassed him, and Chitra's gibe was rubbing salt in his wounds. But he hid his resentment admirably. Throttling his piqued rejoinder, he rose and joined Vikram who crouched a safe distance behind Chitra.

'You can come closer,' invited Chitra. 'Sea snakes are slow and lethargic on land. Like turtles, they turn sluggish when they leave the water.' But the boys stayed put, ignoring her assurances. 'Look at its tail,' continued Chitra. 'It's flattened. The paddle shape is an adaptation to help it move faster in water. The tail distinguishes it from its land cousins and most sea snakes are conspicuously banded like this one.'

Vikram cleared his throat. 'Thanks for the zoology class, Chitra. Now will you back away?'

'Get real,' said Aditya. 'Stop behaving like Wonder Woman.'

'Wonder Woman!' Chitra hissed angrily. She turned away from the snake. 'Is that what you—'

'Look at the snake,' said Vikram urgently. 'It's moving!'

'Of course, it's moving!' snapped Chitra. 'The light is disorienting it. It's headed for the fire. Wonder Woman,' she repeated wrathfully. 'What should I call you, Aditya? Jack-in-the-box? Your stupendous backward leap outdid my jumping toy at home.'

'Cool it, Chitra,' said Vikram earnestly. 'Your feet are planted next to a very dangerous snake.'

'That's exactly what I'm trying to tell you if you will let me. Sea snakes are not dangerous. They are shy, inoffensive creatures. Everyone talks of their venom, not their behaviour. Look—' Chitra's hands reached for the banded coils of the reptile.

'Do not touch, madam!'

Chitra turned. Alex was standing in the firelight, a stern expression on his face.

'I'm just moving it to the side, Alex,' said Chitra. 'It will slither into the fire if I don't.'

'Leave snake alone,' repeated Alex. 'We put out fire instead. No touch snake. I know you like snakes but I not allow.'

'Alex, you've seen me handle sea snakes before.'

'That is with Harry and people who know snakes. Not with me. Boys . . . put out fire, we leave now.'

Vikram and Aditya retrieved the cooking vessels, and giving the snake a wide berth, returned with water and doused the fire.

The snake was like a rope in the sand. Chitra squatted beside it, her shadow falling across its silvery coils.

'Come!' shouted Alex. He was standing in thigh-deep water, holding the Gemini dinghy.

Aditya turned and walked to the sea.

'Come along,' said Vikram, waiting for Chitra.

'It is a beautiful creature, isn't it?' said Chitra, not moving.

'Yes, it is,' agreed Vikram, gazing at its twinkling bands. 'It's beautiful but in a scary sort of way, if you know what I mean.'

Chitra sighed as she rose. 'Scary sort of way,' she echoed, as they trudged to the sea. 'At least you didn't say ugly or repulsive like everybody else. The poor creatures, no one spares them a second glance to admire their beauty and elegance. People just run the moment they see one.'

'Most of us are too frightened to observe the beauty you see,' said Vikram. 'That's why I call it a scary kind of beauty.' He paused at the edge of the beach, looking

out at the moonlit sea. 'From snakes we move on to crocodiles. From a scary reptile to one that is even more so. Of course, both species are beautiful to you, Chitra. But which is more dangerous?'

'Crocodiles.' Chitra replied without hesitation. 'They don't fear us like snakes do. There's no need to worry though, we'll be safe in the dinghy.'

Moonlight flashed on the frothing waves. The sea felt cool as they waded forward. Aditya was already in the dinghy, and Chitra and Vikram clambered in beside him. While Alex pointed the dinghy to the sea, Chitra tugged its starter rope. The motor caught and Alex pulled himself on board. Chitra opened the throttle and the boat surged forward into the silver sea.

CROCODILE CREEK

The sky was cloudless and the moon so bright that it washed the stars away. Alex took over from Chitra and guided the dinghy to the rocks guarding the entry to Lewis Inlet. A wind was blowing across the sea and Vikram was thankful to Chitra for reminding them to wear their jackets. Waves buffeted the dinghy, and a few splashed damply in as they neared the rocks. They quickly passed the rocks, and the inlet lay before them. In the moonlight it was a silver passage of water, blinking between blunt-edged coastlines.

The dinghy passed through the break in the coastline and Vikram heaved a sigh of relief as the wind eased and the water turned calm. A solid wall of silvery mangrove lined the inlet on either side.

Mangroves belong to a specialised group of trees that can tolerate salt water. They do not grow on coastlines exposed to the wind and open sea, but flourish in protected waters like inlets and creeks. In appearance, mangroves can pass as regular trees, but what distinguishes them from all others is their unique root system. Out, at the very edge of land, trees can't survive because the seas flood the area with rising tides. Their roots, which grow downwards into the earth, cannot handle ocean tides, and as a consequence trees are drowned by them. Mangrove trees, however, possess a unique adaptation. Their roots, instead of growing earthward, project skyward from muddy swamps. The roots—called aerial roots—are an essential modification to deal with daily ocean flooding. Here, at Lewis Inlet, where the ocean waters flooded the land, the mangrove grew in huge muddy swamps. Vikram had asked Chitra about the swamps, and she had warned him against entering them unless he had to. 'The roots are like spears in the mud,' she had said. 'They tear at your feet and trip you. You don't want to know how bad they can get. The swamps are a no-go zone. Avoid them at all costs.'

Aditya nudged Vikram, pointing at the water below the Gemini. Vikram gasped. The area beneath the motor seemed to be on fire. There was a bright greenish glow in the dark water.

'Phosphorescence!' cried Vikram. 'Like in Lakshadweep*, remember?'

Aditya nodded.

'It's one of those nights,' shouted Chitra gleefully. 'It doesn't happen every night, but the show is on tonight. Look!' She leaned across the bow of the dinghy and dipped her fingers in the water. Green sparks, like shooting stars, flashed beneath her hand, streaking the darkness below.

---

* Read *Lakshadweep Adventure* to know more about this.

'Any movement or agitation makes the water glow. You can see fish too when they move. Look for flashes in the water.' Sure enough, there were flashes everywhere. Momentary streaks betrayed fish presence in the dark depths of the inlet. Vikram noticed that it was beneath the on-rushing bow of the dinghy that the streaks appeared most frequently.

'That's fish trying to get out of our way,' explained Chitra. 'The dinghy is like a fire-breathing dragon for them. It scares the scales off them.'

'Look there!' shouted Aditya.

He was pointing at a streak of watery yellow that had appeared beside the dinghy. A thin, long fish was pulling ahead of the Gemini underwater. Suddenly five tinier sparks appeared, moving fast. The large glow, with an abrupt burst of speed, flashed after them and the smaller sparks disappeared.

'Wow!' cried Aditya, laughing.

They all understood what they had witnessed. A big fish was chasing smaller ones, and the phosphorescence had revealed their deadly interplay of life and death.

'My dear friend is enjoying himself, I see,' said Chitra, grinning at Vikram's wonderstruck expression. 'And he didn't even want to come.'

Vikram did not reply. He did not want to be reminded. His opposition to the trip was a distant memory. Nothing, not even hostile arrows from the Jarawa, could persuade him to turn back now.

The dinghy travelled about a kilometre into the inlet before Alex eased the throttle and turned its nose to the bank on their right.

Chitra flicked on her torch and flashed it along the bank. 'We're going in now. The creek's here. There's the opening.'

The mangrove wall parted where Chitra shone her torch. A silvery waterway snaked forward through the gap in the forest.

Chitra settled herself at the nose of the boat, and the boys arranged themselves on either side of her. She looked at Vikram and Aditya in turn. 'I'll repeat once more what I told you. This is the last time before we go in, so listen carefully. We're here to search for crocodiles. They're not hard to find as this is their home. This creek is crawling with them. Our plan for locating them is simple: in the dark of the night, light stuns crocodiles. I'll be holding a torch and my beam will search them out. When I find one, I'll lock the beam on its eyes. The moment I do so the crocodile gets paralysed. It can't move. It's true . . . a simple light . . . that's all it takes to immobilise a croc. Shortly after the croc is put out of action, Alex will cut the motor, and we will float towards it. As long as I hold my torch steady, the croc can't move, and we will drift in closer and closer, till the reptile is right beneath us.'

'Within touching distance?' asked Aditya.

'Yes, within touching distance, but I wouldn't try touching it if I were you. Crocs have sharp teeth, and you could lose your hand. Researchers have to measure the crocodile and note its physical characteristics, and to do that they have to get right up close. The crocodile floats in the water while they make their observations, but they don't have much time. The dinghy, though its engine has been cut, drifts towards the crocodile . . . till it finally touches it. When that happens, all hell breaks loose. The spell is broken the moment contact takes place, and the crocodile, alert again, lashes out with its tail and dives into the water. I can't describe the feeling when the crocodile explodes into action. You have to experience it to believe the power the reptile can unleash.'

'What if the dinghy topples?' asked Vikram.

'It won't,' Chitra assured him. 'I've been on several research trips, and not once has that happened.' She looked at the boys. 'The crocs are waiting for us, guys. Are you ready?'

'YES!' cried Vikram and Aditya together.

'Let's go, Alex!' shouted Chitra.

The dinghy slid through the forest parting. The creek was a ribbon of light in the darkness. Its waters were still and glasslike. A shiver of excitement tingled through Vikram. He glanced at Aditya who winked at him.

Chitra flashed her torch along the banks of the creek, skimming the water. Her beam picked out mangrove roots, floating leaves and logs. The sound of the motor echoed harshly in the creek, rebounding off the mangrove. The luminous waterway curved, and the mouth of the creek disappeared behind a screen of mangrove.

Like moths Vikram and Aditya followed Chitra's torch-beam, tracking its every movement as it probed the shadowy recesses of the creek. The three of them spotted the reflection together. Chitra froze the beam, holding the glow it had found. The beam reflected two glimmering spots of light, inches above the surface of the water. Alex

had seen the reflection too, and he released the throttle, slowing the Gemini to a crawl.

No words were spoken. Alex pointed the nose of the dinghy at the twin reflections and cut the engine. In the sudden silence, waves generated by the boat sloshed noisily against the mangrove bank.

The reflections bobbed in the unsettled water, and Chitra held them steady in her beam. They were large—the size of golf balls. As the dinghy drew closer, a scaly head and snout appeared. In the murky water they saw the slit of a mouth and teeth. The dinghy edged nearer, and soon the entire length of the reptile was spread below them.

The crocodile was long, some ten feet or more, estimated Vikram. It floated unmoving, like a thorny log in the water. The beam had cast a spell on the creature. Though its body swayed in the unsteady water there wasn't a single flicker of muscle or scale. It floated docilely, like a fish in an aquarium. The Gemini was moving imperceptibly now, carried forward by its fading momentum. Soon the crocodile was only a few feet from the nose of the dinghy.

The reptile's pole-like frame was thick and powerful. Spiky projections, like the teeth of a saw, crowned its spine. Its tail was long, almost the length of its body. The tail section had similar projections, but they were larger and meaner looking. Vikram held his breath as the boat edged ever closer.

'Watch out,' whispered Chitra, as the dinghy closed in. But Aditya and Vikram continued to lean forward, and the crocodile was barely a foot from them when the dinghy grazed it scales. Despite Chitra's warning, neither of the boys were prepared for what followed.

Like a dormant volcano suddenly erupting, the reptile came alive with a fury that took their breath away. A jet of water shot skywards as the creek exploded and something lifted the Gemini from underneath, heaving it aside. The dinghy rocked wildly, and the teenagers ducked.

'Wow!' screeched Chitra, in delight. Her torch, now inside the boat, illuminated their faces. Chitra's eyes were shining and there was a rapturous expression on her face. Aditya's eyes were glazed, but he was laughing. Vikram didn't know it, but his fists were clenched, and his brow was soaked with sweat. He was laughing too, and his eyes were glowing as brightly as those of the crocodile.

The thunderous energy displayed by the armoured reptile had been breathtaking. From paralysed dormancy to frenzied motion, it had all taken place in a fraction of a second, and the reptile was gone.

'Fantastic,' whispered Vikram reverently.

'Great, isn't it?' gushed Chitra. 'Want some more?'

'You bet,' replied Aditya, his face shining.

Alex was already revving the Gemini. He turned its nose around, pointing it up the creek once more. Chitra handed Aditya the torch and in quick time, after just a couple of twists in the winding creek, two pairs of eyes glowed lamp-like in the water. Aditya trapped them both in his beam. Alex cut the engine once more and the Gemini drifted towards the pair of crocodiles while waves crashed noisily against the banks.

The crocodiles were smaller, about half the size of the monster they had seen earlier. They lay partly submerged in the water, balanced on mangrove roots. Their skin was a murky grey in the torchlight, and their teeth flashed ivory white. On this occasion the reptiles did not wait till the dinghy floated up to them. They exploded into furious action when the Gemini was still metres away. Roots shook and water spouted as they flashed into the water, vanishing in its murky depths.

It was Vikram's turn to hold the torch next. Adrenaline pumped in his veins as he watched the beam pierce the tangle of roots at the water's edge. The circle of brightness skimmed over leaves, twigs and dead branches, illuminating dark, forbidding banks. Chitra spotted the glitter first and Vikram immediately retracted the beam, trapping the fiery orbs she had seen. There was only one crocodile, and it floated statue-like as the dinghy drifted closer. Once more it broke into explosive motion when the rubber hull of the Gemini grazed it. The awesome display of power was addictive, and neither Chitra nor the boys could get enough of it.

The creek twisted and turned as they motored deeper into the forest. The moon was their only point of reference. It floated one moment before them and at the next curve it swung away to the side; sometimes it shone like a searchlight from behind.

Just as the forest was dark, the sky was ablaze with milky radiance. Its light illumined the snaking waterway, rendering it a ghostly silver. The setting was beautiful and wild. An incomparable wilderness, as Chitra had said.

Crocodile picking was easy. They halted several times on finding the reptiles. After many exhilarating encounters, when they had penetrated deep into the creek, it split into two waterways.

Alex released the throttle and halted the dinghy. 'Go back?' he enquired.

'NO!' exclaimed the teenagers together.

Alex's teeth gleamed in the moonlight as he smiled.

'Move over, Alex,' said Chitra. 'I want the controls.'

'So do I,' blurted Aditya.

'Maybe missy drive, short distance only. Then turn back. No, Aditya, sorry. You no practice, I give you daytime.'

Chitra switched places with Alex, and the journey continued. Choosing the right fork, she directed the boat along the flashing waterway. Aditya held the torch and searched the banks. Chitra drove slowly to start with, but her confidence quickly grew, and soon the Gemini was racing through the water. Vikram was uneasy at first. But his concern eased as Chitra displayed fine control, negotiating the curves expertly. He and the others scanned the banks and the water for reflections. Chitra gunned the boat faster. Vikram smiled as he gazed at the moonlit shore. The similarities between her and Aditya were unending. She was behaving exactly as Aditya would have, testing the boundaries of her skill.

The creek had begun to narrow, but Chitra did not lessen her speed. The banks twisted as another curve appeared on the mercury-like highway. Vikram looked at Alex, wondering whether he would caution Chitra, but he didn't, and she maintained her speed as she negotiated the curve.

Clasping a tie-rope, Vikram saw the silver crescent of their river-path emerge around a sharp curve. Chitra must have been aware that her speed was excessively high because she didn't pursue a tight turn that would have held the dinghy to the centre of the waterway. Instead she widened her turn, moving to the far bank. Chitra, like the rest of the occupants of the dinghy, wasn't prepared for an obstruction beside the bank. She might easily have avoided it if her speed was more controlled, but her on-the-brink velocity allowed no margin for swerves or alteration of direction.

Chitra was left with no choice but to collide with the obstruction. 'WATCH OUT!' she yelled, and the next thing her companions knew was that the dinghy had come to a sudden halt . . . but not them. They flew forward, pitching head first into the silver waters of the creek.

CHITRA

Of all the occupants in the dinghy Chitra was the best prepared for the collision. She clung to the throttle during the impact, but when the dinghy started to keel, she kicked herself away, acutely aware of the spinning motor blades.

She hit the water hard. A cold darkness engulfed her as the force of her impact carried her under. She couldn't see, the blackout around her was total. Her lungs were contracting—she needed to breathe. Her stomach churned as blind panic seized her. She kicked hard, but even after several energetic strokes the darkness remained. Her heart suddenly lurched—her hand had brushed something. Was it a crocodile? No, the material was slimy and soft. It was mud. She had been swimming downwards.

Chitra reversed direction and instantly spied a pale luminescence. Her lungs were straining. She swam forcefully, and the luminescence turned radiant. Her head broke free into a blaze of dazzling light. Her chest heaved as she sucked warm, humid air. But something hard and

abrasive was moving along her body, tearing at her skin. It wasn't a crocodile as her fearful mind instinctively apprehended. It was wood. Shadows snaked everywhere about her. She had surfaced amidst mangrove roots.

The water was shallow. Her feet were snagged amidst roots and mud. Chitra gasped and panted, regaining her breath. With only her head out of the water she stared at the scene of the accident.

Several torches shone in the darkness. Strange, she thought, wondering where so many had sprung from. Then her eyes took in the larger picture, and she realised what had happened. The obstruction she had smashed into was a dungi. There were men standing on its hull, and they were helping Vikram into the boat. Further down, Aditya was pulling himself in, rocking the dungi from side-to-side. The Gemini had been flipped upside down, and Alex was standing in hip-deep water holding on to it. Chitra was about to swim to Alex, but the dull reflection of torchlight on steel held her back. Two of the men in the dungi had guns, and one of the guns was pointed at Alex.

Chitra counted four men in the dungi. At first, she supposed they were coastguard officers or naval intelligence personnel, but then she spotted the tall man called Patrick. There was an angry snarl on Patrick's face. Alex had branded Patrick a criminal, and the weapon in his hand seemed to confirm it. As she gazed disbelievingly at the torchlit tableau it struck her that her absence had not been noticed. She had been overlooked during the mêlée following the accident. The presence of weapons spurred Chitra to action.

Turning, she sought the shelter of the mangrove. She clambered over roots and hid behind the trunk of the nearest tree. No one shouted, no one turned to look. Instead, everyone was staring at Aditya who was making a thunderous fuss in the dungi. He was standing beside Vikram, shouting deafeningly, a furious expression on his face. A gun was pointed squarely at his chest, yet Aditya continued to rant.

Aditya seemed to be beside himself with rage. He was waving a fist beneath the nose of the man threatening him with the gun. It was when Chitra noticed that Aditya's antics had captured everyone's attention that she grasped his intent. Could it be that he was presenting her an opportunity to escape? Chitra did not linger to find out. Turning her back on her friends, she slipped further into the mangrove.

The going wasn't easy. Chitra was under no illusions of the task confronting her. A mess of roots surrounded her. Thick, bruising, skin-gouging roots unfolded in knotted bunches between the trees. Strewn between the roots was waist-deep mud that sucked at her like quicksand. Mud and roots consolidated to create a formidable obstacle course. Adding to her predicament was the enshrouding darkness, which increased the difficulty several-fold.

Grasping blindly at slimy roots, Chitra dragged herself forward. She staggered and stumbled in the mud. There were roots everywhere. The shadowy outlines of those which rose above the mud were vaguely visible, but the ones submerged beneath were undetectable, and they continuously tripped Chitra, often pitching her face down in the mud. The roots raked her jeans and ripped her skin, drawing blood from her legs and hands.

It wasn't long before Chitra was battered, bloodied and coated with mud from head to toe. But she kept going, ploughing deeper into the mangrove. When torch beams began to probe the creek waters Chitra knew that the search for her had begun. Ignoring her wounds, she doubled her efforts. A torch beam infiltrated the mangrove, moving slowly from tree to tree. Chitra ducked when the beam neared her. It flitted over her, and Chitra's eyes followed it as it illuminated a maze of trunks, roots and mud. It briefly lit two circles of red as it arced away from her. Chitra's breath froze.

There was a crocodile in the mangrove.

Chitra looked around desperately. The swamp was dark and shadowy. There could be several crocodiles here. She turned and gazed at the lights on the creek. The dungi assured her safety, at least from crocodiles. All she had to do was retrace her path and give herself up.

Chitra breathed deeply. She couldn't allow the presence of a crocodile to break her. Not after her stay at the 'Crocodile Bank', in Chennai. It was at the Crocodile Bank that she had decided to study reptiles. But how could she if she was going to run away from them? Wouldn't she be confronted with similar situations when she researched them? Chitra gritted her teeth. Crocodiles were not going to turn her away. Her swamp trek tonight would be a test of her temperament.

Crouching, Chitra moved on, her senses on high alert. She hunched low, slipping and crawling over the roots. The going was painful, difficult and nerve-racking. More than crocodiles, it was the mud that troubled Chitra. Though now only thigh-deep it still concealed endless walls of roots that tripped and tore at her. There was mud in her eyes, mud on her face, and her hair was cloaked so hopelessly with muck and slime that she wondered whether she would ever be able to wash it clean again.

Chitra plodded on, moving deeper inland. The mud would have to turn shallow at some point, when the swamp yielded to dry land. But the conditions were against her—the tide was high. The wetness and the mud stretched far into the forest, and it was a long time before it began to lessen.

Just as the going turned easy, Chitra heard a shout. A man was gibbering at the water's edge and shining his torch along the creek bank. His beam illuminated the roots of a nearby mangrove tree. Had he discovered her trail?

The mud was only knee-deep now and Chitra quickened her pace. But her leg snagged in hidden roots, and she fell heavily. It was as she scrabbled to her knees in the mud that she heard the sound. It was a soft plop followed by a distinct slithering.

Chitra froze.

Shafts of moonlight lanced the mangrove canopy, casting shadows and pockmarking the mud. The slithering sound repeated itself and Chitra saw a shadow move.

It could only be a crocodile, and if she guessed correctly, the reptile was nearby. Chitra heard more shouts from the creek. The torches were now probing deeper into the swamp, following her trail.

The slither sounded briefly and halted. Chitra breathed deeply. Reaching for her pouch, she extracted her torch. She was reluctant to switch it on as it would reveal her location to the men. But it was her only defence against the crocodile, and if she was forced to turn it on, she would.

Chitra's heart beat so loudly that she was sure the crocodile could hear it. Strangely, she experienced not the slightest fear. Instead, she sensed a heightened awareness. She could hear the men at the creek, and she knew they were wading forward. She also heard the faint plop of air oozing through the mud and the slither of a moving reptile.

Chitra flicked on her torch. The direction of her beam was fairly accurate because it illuminated the undulating tail of a crocodile. Chitra swept her beam forward, settling it on the reptile's face so that its eyes shone back at her. Loud shouts erupted behind her, and torches shone deep into the swamp.

Chitra held her beam on the reptile's eyes. The crocodile was a full-grown specimen. Like an armoured tank it crouched frozen in the mud. Had it been lying in her path waiting for her, or had it simply been trying to get away from her? Chitra couldn't tell, but it didn't matter now; her torch beam had stunned the reptile.

Her pursuers were shouting in Hindi, ordering her to halt. Chitra skirted around the stunned reptile holding her beam steady on its eyes. The shouts from the shore were getting shriller. A gun exploded, ripping the forest silence. Birds squawked in alarm, and Chitra heard the sound of a bullet smacking into a tree. Her beam wavered and lost contact with the crocodile's eyes. Mud churned as the animal snapped from its spell. Another shot rang out, and Chitra ducked. Her torch illuminated the crocodile once more. The reptile was sliding away from her, shooting through the mud.

Switching off her torch, Chitra slipped it back into her pouch. Furious shouting roared from the creek. The voices belonged to her friends. There was anger in their cries. They were yelling at the men, warning them not to shoot.

The guns turned silent. The swamp glowed eerily as beams of light explored its gloomy depths. Chitra hunched low as she slipped from tree to tree. The going had eased now. Though mud still squelched beneath her it was barely ankle-deep and there were far fewer roots to deal with. The shouting from behind was loud and strident, commanding her to halt.

The ground was turning dry beneath Chitra's feet. Mangrove was yielding to other trees. When she passed a bank of banana-like pandanus trees she abandoned her crouching stance and stood erect. Vegetation was thick everywhere about her, and the torchlight from behind no longer shone through.

Chitra turned and parted the brush behind. The distant creek shone like a silver thread. The torch beams had advanced into the swamp. But though they probed the forest, Chitra could see that they were stationary.

Voices percolated through the intervening swamp. A discussion was in progress. Snatches of conversation trickled audibly through the forest silence. One of the pursuers was inclined to push on while the other wanted to abandon the search till morning. Shortly, another voice called authoritatively from the creek. The argument was cut short and Chitra heaved a sigh of relief as the torches turned and retreated to the dungi.

Chitra's teeth began to chatter. The night was cool, and her clothes were soaked. Like a sticky shroud, mud smeared every part of her clothing, face and hair. It felt as if someone had thrown her under a car. She was sore, bruised and bleeding from several cuts. She had managed to escape, but what now?

Presently, she heard the sound of motors. Engines boomed in the forest silence. Both the dungi and the Gemini were on the move. Listening to the deafening reverberations, it struck Chitra that the men must have heard their approach long before she took that disastrous high-speed turn. She wondered whether they had deliberately parked their dungi near the creek bank. If she had not taken the turn so fast, the Gemini would have held its bearing at the centre of the creek, and they might have motored past without seeing the boat at all.

But why had the men attempted to hide? What were they up to? They were armed and dangerous and had taken the extreme step of shooting at her. She and her friends had stumbled on to something they shouldn't have; something so secretive that Patrick and his men were even willing to kill to safeguard.

Chitra followed the progress of the boats by the ringing beat of their motors. When their tone changed and their sound grew muffled, she knew that the boats had altered direction, looping about the numerous turns in the creek. There were several tonal shifts in the sound, and as time passed, the noise turned progressively dimmer until both the engines were suddenly cut off.

The boats hadn't gone far.

Chitra shivered as she waited in the dark, but the engines did not restart. Could it be that they had a camp nearby and that the boats had halted there? If that were the case, she had better keep going. She couldn't afford to halt here; they would come for her in the morning.

Turning, Chitra switched on her torch. She walked slowly, parting underbrush and ducking beneath creepers. Wind sighed through the canopy, showering leaves to the ground. Trees heaved, their branches rippling in the moonlight. The forest was alive with sounds. Lizards called loudly with their rhythmic, plop-plop clicks. The scaly creatures were awake and hunting, and so were owls. She often heard the croak-like calls of the Andaman Wood Owl.

Chitra was glad to discover that the forest held no fears for her. The dark and the shadows did not trouble her, neither did the unseen rustle and slither from behind bushes and vegetation. She was aware that animals of the Andaman forests were mostly harmless. The cat family carnivores—tigers, leopards and lions—were absent. None had managed the journey from the mainland to the islands. There were deer, pigs, mice, rabbits, monitor lizards and plenty of other creatures—none of which troubled Chitra.

But it wasn't only animals that Chitra had to contend with. There were humans in this forest too. An ancient people lived here; a people whom she respected and was genuinely afraid of. Yet, though deep in Jarawa territory,

she took comfort from the fact that the Jarawa were not known to be abroad at this time of the night.

Progress was not easy. The forest was thick and there were no paths. Her torch helped considerably as she searched her way through the shadowed maze on the forest floor. Her jacket and jeans, though cold and wet, protected her from the undergrowth. But the exposed skin on her hands, already bloodied by the mangrove, was pierced and torn by thorns and creepers.

Chitra wasn't wearing a watch, and she lost track of time. It was after an hour, or possibly two, of plodding progress, that she suddenly felt herself treading water. There were no trees and she could see the stars. Chitra looked about her. She was standing at the edge of a clearing. The surface of the clearing was smooth, and like a mirror it reflected the moon and the stars. Suddenly the inverted bowl of stars began to blur and Chitra heard flapping sounds. She stepped back in alarm. It was as if a cloud was rising from the clearing. Chitra heard squawks and piercing calls. Birds! Chitra's heart, having leapt into her mouth, settled shakily back in her chest. She had arrived at the edge of a pond and had startled a flock of birds that had been sleeping in its waters.

It was a large pond, and a circle of trees rimmed its border. While Chitra stood waiting for her heartbeat to normalise, the birds slowly returned, dropping one by one from the sky and settling in the water. Chitra stood for several minutes, enjoying the unbroken view of the heavens and their twinkling reflection. The dense forest had oppressed her. The wide spaces of sky lifted her spirits, and the friendly presence of birds soothed her frayed nerves.

Chitra needed a place to halt, and this seemed as charming and safe a spot as any. Switching on her torch, she shone its beam on the trees, setting off another flurry of wingbeats as the birds panicked and took off again.

Ignoring them, she searched for a suitable tree to spend the night on. She selected one with a massive trunk. Several branches forked from its trunk, and Chitra's eyes settled on a broad branch that fused with the trunk at a safe height from the ground. Clambering up wasn't difficult, and Chitra was thankful to discover a hollow at the crook of the branch. Gathering leaves she heaped them in the hollow, cushioning its hard edges.

The birds had settled once more, and silence returned to the forest. Her clothes had dried to some extent but were still clammy and cold. Her waterproof jacket, however, had dried out completely and provided welcome warmth. Uncorking one of the bottles from her belt, she drank deeply. She was safe for the night. Her pursuers wouldn't come till daylight. She could rest till then. Her eyelids were drooping. A large bat flew past overhead, and she heard the call of a hawk owl. The last images she saw were of stars, before she drifted into an uneasy sleep.

IN THE FOREST

It was the cold that woke Chitra. Although her clothes had dried out, they weren't thick enough to keep out the morning chill. Her cheeks had lost sensation. Running her fingers across her face, she discovered that it wasn't just her cheeks that she couldn't feel; even her nose and ears seemed to have iced solid.

Fatigue and overpowering sleepiness had insulated her earlier, but now, with her waking, her teeth began to chatter. She dug her palms into her armpits and squeezed her legs against her chest. The cold was too intense for her to fall asleep again. Fortunately, a dull light was diffusing the sky. Stars were winking out in the great emptiness above, and though the sun had not yet risen, the trees were alive with song as birds greeted the coming of a new day.

Shivering, Chitra looked about her. The pond she had splashed into the previous night glimmered faintly, reflecting traces of light in the sky. Several duck-like shadows were floating on its waters. There was something familiar about the birds, and despite the murky light she identified their fuzzy outlines and dull plumage. The birds were teals—Andaman teals.

From above, she heard a flurry of discordant musical calls. Though the cacophony sounded like the collective warblings of a flock of birds, Chitra knew otherwise. Just one bird—the racket-tailed drongo—was responsible for the noise. The large black bird, with trailing tail feathers, was the noisy and delightful mimic of the Andaman forests. Looking up, she spotted it in the high branches, joyfully greeting the emerging sun.

A flock of glossy starlings, flashing dark, shiny feathers, settled quietly above the drongo. From the corner of her eye, Chitra glimpsed what looked like a falling stone. Turning, she saw a kingfisher drop noiselessly to the pond waters. But before piercing its surface, the bird banked and broke its descent. After hovering briefly, exposing bright blue wings, it flew to a tree on the far side of the pond and settled.

Chitra blinked. Had she spotted movement below the kingfisher? At first, all she saw were shadows, but the strengthening light soon revealed a herd of deer. A handsome stag, sporting large antlers, was staring silently across the water, while three other smaller deer, minus the crowning headgear, were drinking. Grass grew along the edge of the pond, and after satisfying their thirst, the animals nibbled on the clumps at their feet.

Chitra started when she heard a rustling below her. Her breath caught in her throat when she spotted a log-like shadow not far from the tree she was perched on.

A crocodile!

The reptile was crouched a short distance from her tree, alongside the pebbly bank of the pond. Saltwater crocodiles never venture far from the sea. The creature's presence indicated she wasn't as far inland as she thought she was. It could be that the creek, or one of its many bends, passed near the clearing.

Unable to tear her eyes away, Chitra stared at the crocodile, but the spell was broken when the Andaman teals fluttered heavily into the air. Her eyes swept the pond, searching for what might have disturbed them, and her breath caught once more. The deer were no longer there. Instead, the bushes on the opposite bank had parted, and she saw two men emerge.

'*Jarawa!*' was the first terrifying thought that sprang to her mind. But the men weren't dark-skinned and neither were they naked. They were dressed in trousers and their shirts hung to their knees. One was carrying a machete and the other had a handgun tucked in his belt. Chitra's throat turned dry as she stared in horror at them. She had expected them to come, but not as early as the crack of dawn.

The teals circled and flew away. Chitra turned statue-still. The chill of the morning was forgotten as she stared at the men. One of them dug into his pocket and offered the other a cigarette. Chitra waited only till a match was struck and their heads were bowed. Slipping over the edge of the branch, she clung to creepers and lowered herself to the ground.

The men puffed away.

Hunching low, Chitra turned to the forest. As she started forward, she heard a pattering sound. Stifling a scream, Chitra took three rapid backward steps and stumbling, fell.

The crocodile!

Its presence had completely slipped her mind. The reptile was poised just a few metres from her.

The morning calm was shattered by loud shouts.

Chitra lunged to her feet and ran.

'HALT!' roared a voice, in Hindi. 'Halt! Or I shoot!'

Chitra ducked under a branch and dashed into the forest. Trees banded tightly about her, and leaves crackled beneath her pounding feet. A gunshot rang out, and birds squawked in alarm. Chitra cringed as a bullet ripped through bushes and thudded into a tree not far from her. She gasped and turned. But she couldn't see the men. A tangled mess of trunks, branches and underbrush screened her from them. The hammering in her chest eased—if she couldn't see them, they too couldn't see her. The men were shooting blind.

It helped that the pond lay between her and her pursuers. They would have to skirt around it before beginning the chase. The head start was crucial. Chitra was a good runner and was confident of maintaining her lead. But though staying ahead did not pose a problem, losing the men was another matter altogether. An ankle-deep carpet of leaves blanketed the forest floor, rendering silent movement impossible. Though her pursuers might not be able to see her, the sound of her passage would broadcast her whereabouts.

As she ran, it struck Chitra that except for the previous night, never before had bullets been fired at her. Surprisingly, the realisation bolstered her instead of dispiriting her. The undergrowth had protected her then, and since the area she was running in was thickly forested, it would continue to shield her from bullets.

Chitra lost track of time as she ran. Direction, too, was something she had no clue of. The rising sun was her only point of reference. Though screened by the overhead canopy, its glow was discernible through the branches. But never did its glow remain in the same place. Sometimes it shone to her left, and when she changed direction—which she frequently did—it shifted to her right. Often it disappeared behind her and Chitra wondered whether she was running in circles. But direction was of little consequence. It was staying ahead of her pursuers that mattered. Thankfully, she maintained her original lead, and comfortably so.

Sweat poured from Chitra, and it wasn't long before a keen thirst built within her, but she couldn't risk a halt for a drink. Though bullets were no longer being fired at her, the sound of pursuit was relentless. Minutes slipped quickly by till Chitra wasn't sure whether it was an hour or two that the men had been chasing her.

Chitra often wondered where her meandering flight was leading her. Would she stumble on to a creek? Would she arrive at the sea? Or would she burst on to a Jarawa settlement? But the terrain about Chitra remained unchanged. There was no muddy water to indicate the presence of a creek, no boom of surf to announce the sea, and neither did a Jarawa settlement appear. Instead, the forest seemed to go on forever. Although Chitra did not want to stop, as time went by her throat grew unbearably dry, and it was the desperate need for a drink that eventually forced her to halt.

Breathing heavily, she extracted the unopened bottle from her belt and sucked greedily. Two deep gulps were sufficient to exhaust its contents. It was as she returned the bottle to her belt that she spied movement. Dropping to the ground she ducked behind a tree. Despite the water, her throat turned dry once more. She had spotted a flash of colour. No animal in the Andaman Islands was coloured blue. She had miscalculated badly—her pursuers were far closer than she had expected.

Chitra shrank against the trunk she crouched behind. Although her pursuer was close, the flash had appeared to one side of her. If he kept going the man would pass without noticing her presence; the dense undergrowth would take care of that. But the man halted. The sounds of his progress suddenly ceased. Chitra held her breath. He couldn't possibly have seen her. But then why had he halted?

In the silence Chitra heard a distant crashing sound, as if someone or something was blundering through the undergrowth. Was the pursuer in front waiting for his companion to catch up? Chitra could only guess.

Time passed.

The throbbing in Chitra's calves and thighs eased. A flock of parakeets squawked noisily, and she saw a flutter of green as they sped through the trees. A faint whirring prompted Chitra to turn, and she spotted a speeding black object weaving through the trees. One glimpse was enough.

So familiar was she with this bird that the momentary flash was all she required to identify it as a swiftlet.

A sense of unease pervaded Chitra as the heavy tramp of the second man drew closer. Why had the first man halted? Why would he, when he knew that by doing so, he was ceding her an opportunity to increase her lead? The termination of the chase didn't make sense unless . . . unless the man had been tracking her by sound and not by sight. There was a growing certainty in Chitra's mind that the man had been tracking her by the clamour of her flight. Whichever way she looked at it, it made sense. In a dense forest like this, visibility was poor and unreliable, but sound was consistent, providing positive direction. The man had been following a trail of sound, and when that had ceased, he had concluded she had halted. He was convinced that she was hiding and had altered his strategy accordingly.

Presently, all sounds of movement ceased, and Chitra heard voices. Though she strained her ears, the distance rendered the conversation inaudible. Dropping her head, Chitra surveyed the tree she hid behind. Thick roots projecting from its trunk doubled its girth. Chitra eased herself to the edge of the massive roots and peered around them.

At first, all she saw was a screen of vegetation. But shortly, through the mass of leaves and branches, she spotted shadows. The shadows were stationary. A fresh course of action was being plotted. Chitra considered the possibility of stealing away while they were thus occupied. But when she looked at the carpet of leaves surrounding her, she held back.

Minutes later, she heard the shuffle of feet on leaves. The shadows were separating. One was drifting to the left, but the other was tramping towards her part of the forest. Chitra watched the approaching man. He was moving slowly, examining the vegetation about him. It was a cat-and-mouse game now. The breathless chase through the forest had been abandoned.

After a minute of watching the unnerving approach of the man, an unexpected noise startled Chitra. There was a sharp crackling of leaves, which ceased as abruptly as it began. The forest turned silent as both men halted. The undergrowth rustled once more; a brief shuffle followed by silence. The men called to one another, and the one that had been moving away came running to join his companion.

Chitra identified the source of the sound the second time she heard it. There was something in the underbrush, and it wasn't far from her. It was dark, not particularly tall, and too squat to be a human being. A pig . . . yes . . . it was a wild boar. It was standing crouched, peering through the shrubbery at the men.

The pig was too close for comfort. Clenching her fists Chitra fumed at the animal. If the men came to investigate it, they would surely see her.

'*Shoo!*' she mouthed wordlessly at the pig. '*Go away!* Get out of here!'

But the pig didn't budge. It froze instead, adopting the outline of a big black boulder.

The men crept forward.

Chitra looked desperately about her.

A swiftlet sped past, but she didn't pay it any attention.

The shelter of the tree roots wasn't enough, she had to find a better hiding place. But where? There were only trees about her; trees and their serpentine roots.

Chitra prayed that the pig would move and reveal itself for what it was, but the animal stubbornly refused.

The men drew closer.

Two more swiftlets flitted by.

Chitra's eyes followed them despairingly and she blinked. The birds had abruptly vanished into the ground. Another swiftlet appeared and vanished too. It was as if the earth had gobbled them up. Chitra stared at the spot where they had disappeared, and then she saw it.

A cave!

There was a swiftlet cave barely ten metres from her. Amidst the tangle of roots on the forest floor yawned a big black hole. Now that she saw it, she wondered how she had missed it. Chitra's heart beat faster.

The cave!

It was a perfect hiding place. She couldn't have asked for anything better. There was no time for indecision. The cave was her best bet . . . but the leaves.

Chitra groaned silently.

Several metres of leaf-littered floor lay between her and the cave. The men would surely hear her when she trod on them. But luck favoured Chitra. One of the numerous roots of the tree she hid behind snaked towards the cave. The twisting, bark-less surface offered her a raised path, clear of the leaf litter, almost to the foot of the slit-like opening of the cave.

The men were drawing closer, their attention fixed on the area the pig was hiding in. Soon, there was a snort followed by the drum of running feet.

Chitra chose that moment to break for the cave.

On hands and knees, she scrambled across the massive root. Chitra was an agile girl. She moved fast, soundlessly covering the length of the root. But the root suddenly ended, terminating short of the cave. It was too late to turn back. Chitra had committed herself the moment she had mounted the root. She rose and leapt. The unforgiving leaf carpet crackled loudly, once and then a second time, before she launched herself into the dark opening.

grasped her torch she couldn't summon the courage to switch it on.

Stones trickled softly again.

It was like footsteps—footsteps in the dark. Gravel and stone rolled quietly. Chitra worked on her fingers. She had to switch her torch on. Suddenly, she sensed something behind her. Something cold snaked across her stomach. She shrieked a terror-stricken scream. But she never heard her scream; another cold, slimy object was pressing hard on her mouth, muffling her terror. Chitra felt herself being lifted off the ground. She closed her eyes, not resisting. Deep tremors racked her body as she was half-pushed, half-carried into an area of total darkness.

Chitra's recollections of what followed were hazy. Numb with shock, she only partly registered what was happening about her. From a distance, it seemed, she heard the sound of something thudding against the ground. She heard voices. Men were speaking in Hindi. Questions were being raised, angry answers were returned, and though Chitra could clearly hear the exchange, the words were lost on her. Her mind had retreated into a shell.

Chitra's abiding memory of the incident was the clammy, soaking feeling of sweat and the cold wet hand that pressed against her mouth, never letting go. The cave passage she had been borne to was warm and airless. But it wasn't just the stifling conditions of the cave that fuelled her sweat; fear contributed far more.

Chitra lost hope of her torment ever ending as she stood in the suffocating chamber of the cave. But end it did when the voices finally subsided. The hand fell from her mouth, and Chitra felt herself being released. The darkness about her was so profuse that she saw nothing of her captor's departure. Quiet footsteps were the only indication.

Chitra breathed deeply. There were swiftlets flying about her. She couldn't see them, but their squeaking and chirruping was unmistakable. The swiftlet symphony comforted Chitra. As time passed, the terror of the dark and the horror of the clammy touch receded. She regained her composure as her mind stabilised, exhibiting a welcome willingness to return to normal.

Though her eyes were thoroughly adjusted to the dark, she still couldn't see. She must have been carried to some deep cavern of the cave. Even shadows were absent. Having lost her torch earlier, when the clammy hands had grabbed her, she sensibly decided to stay put. Moving blind in an unknown cave was foolish and dangerous.

It wasn't long before she heard footsteps again. There were voices too. A light appeared. A dazzling beam was moving in her direction. The beam halted beside her, illuminating the ground she stood on. Then it was raised and directed at her face. Chitra blinked and shielded her eyes.

'Who are you?' asked a voice in Hindi.

Chitra nervously spoke her name.

The voice, a pleasant conversational one, queried why people were chasing her. Chitra heaved a sigh of relief. These men were not her pursuers.

Chitra replied truthfully. Explaining the entire sequence of events, she began with their encounter with Patrick's boat and continued without a break until her blind leap into the cave. She finished by asking about the men chasing her. 'They have gone,' replied the man briefly. 'I told them we were the only people in the cave.'

There were shadows behind the man. His talk with Chitra completed, he turned to them. A whispered conversation followed. Two shadows then walked forward, switching on torches as they passed Chitra. Chitra's gaze followed their beams, and she gasped suddenly, her breath choking.

She understood in a flash why the men had come to this cave.

The beams of their torches revealed birds, hundreds of them, circling the darkness. It wasn't the sight of the birds that distressed her, it was what she could see on the ground. The cave floor was littered with nests. The beautiful half-moon nests of the swiftlets had been hacked off the cave walls. And crawling amidst the carnage of broken nests, Chitra saw tiny birds. The hatchlings . . . recently born babies that couldn't fly . . . they had tumbled to the ground along with the nests. A chill crept through Chitra. These men were poachers; they had come here to pillage swiftlet nests.

'You don't like this,' spoke the voice of the torch bearer.

Chitra did not reply. Instead, she stepped back, grabbing the torch from the man's hand. She directed its beam upwards, along the cave walls.

The nesting colony had been destroyed. All that remained was smudges, pearly in the torchlight, where the swiftlets' saliva had cemented their nests to the wall. A cloud of birds was circling above. Their distress was palpable, and the enclosed area of the cave reverberated with their clicks.

Four bamboo poles were resting against the walls. Their purpose was obvious; they had been used to get at the nests. On the ground, the men who had walked past her were heaping the fallen nests in a cloth bag. Tiny hatchlings were crawling pathetically between their feet, and surprisingly the men were gently pushing the birds aside, taking care not to step on them.

'Those hatchlings will die,' said Chitra.

'I know that,' said the man standing beside Chitra. 'We do not wish to kill them. It is unfortunate, but we need the nests and they are in the way.' Though Chitra could not see, she sensed that the man had shrugged in the darkness.

'Couldn't you have waited till the hatchlings were big enough to fly?' asked Chitra. 'Why did you have to break the nests now?'

'Somebody else would have got here first. This cave is known to several people. Those who come first reap the nests. We didn't get any nests last season, somebody else was here before us. This time we have got them.'

A fierce anger was building inside Chitra, but she controlled herself. Only her heightened breathing betrayed her rage. The precariousness of her situation was not lost on Chitra. She was alone with three unknown men in a cave in the middle of a forest. She was at their mercy.

'Why did you help me?' she enquired, changing the subject.

'We heard you in the forest. I climbed out of the cave and saw you hiding. I saw the men following you. Those men are bad. We have seen them before, and we know that they kill. So we hid you when they entered. They didn't believe us when we told them we were alone in the cave. They said that they had heard someone jump into the cave, and I told them that it was one of my men they heard. I invited them to check the cave to satisfy their doubts. Borrowing my torch, they searched from the cave entrance. This part of the cave is well hidden, and you cannot find it unless you know about it. They gave up soon and left after warning us to hand you over if we found you. They must still be searching for you.'

Chitra breathed a little easier. The awful spectacle of broken nests and the doomed hatchlings had sped shivers of dread down her spine, and she had wondered whether she had leapt from the frying pan into a fire. But although these men were poachers, they were not killers. They might have taken the lives of many hundred birds, yet they had saved hers.

But in spite of their having protected her, Chitra found it difficult to respect them. The edible nest swiftlet colony had been destroyed. How could they? Her entire being felt revolted.

So distraught was Chitra that she didn't want to look into the cave. Shutting out the mayhem behind her she turned to the man. 'Who are these men and why are they chasing me?' she asked.

'I don't personally know them,' replied the man. 'All I know is that they have a camp about two hours from here.

Only a few people who venture into this area know of their camp. No one goes there. They leave us alone and we leave them alone.'

'You have never been to their camp?' asked Chitra.

'No. Nor do I want to.'

'Will you help me get there?'

There was silence for a moment, then: 'You believe your captured friends are being held there?'

'Yes.'

There was silence again before the man spoke. 'When we leave, I can select a route that passes that way. I can take you near their camp, but that is all I will do. Do not expect us to help you rescue your friends.'

'No, I shall not,' said Chitra. 'It will be enough if you get me there. I will be grateful for the favour.'

'Here, this is yours,' said the man. He thrust something into her hand and walked away.

It was her torch. Chitra switched it on. The man she had been speaking to stooped beside his companions, helping them with their grisly task. All the nests had been collected from the cave floor and the men were fastening the strings of the cloth bags they had been stuffed into.

Chitra's heart went out to the birds as she shone her torch along the cave walls. How often had their homes been ransacked? This wasn't the first time that their eggs had been destroyed and their young ones doomed. And this wouldn't be the last.

If only their nests weren't edible. If only they would learn to use twigs and bark, like other birds did. Humans would leave them alone then. It was the rare gift nature had

Chitra was the first to scramble to the top. The bags containing the nests were sent up next. Then the others followed.

After the muggy confines of the cave, the forest was cool and refreshing, like air conditioning. Shadows and dappled sunlight fell about them once more. Birdcalls rang everywhere, and there was the hum of crickets.

One of the poachers crossed to a bush and extracted a pair of backpacks. Unstrapping the first, he pulled out a water bottle and offered it to Chitra. Smiling, she accepted it and drank gratefully.

The other backpack contained tiffin boxes. They were opened and spread on the ground. Chitra's stomach rumbled when she saw potato subzi and chapatis inside. The contents of the tiffin boxes were divided and distributed equally.

Birds flew past as they ate. Most were swiftlets—birds that no longer had a home. The cooling Chitra had experienced after stepping out of the cave soon wore off, and sweat moistened her brow once more. The mini meal was consumed quickly, and though Chitra's hunger was only partially sated, she felt better. After drinking a final round of water everyone rose to their feet. Chitra was glad to discover that the men were as eager to get going as she was. The thin-faced man shouldered the nest bags, and the backpacks were distributed between the other two.

A kilometre-crunching pace was set. Despite being taller and having longer legs, Chitra had to strain herself to keep up with the men. Sweat flowed freely once more, and the familiar sticky feeling spread everywhere.

No words were exchanged. Chitra believed that the silence was deliberate. There had been no attempt to find out who she was or where she came from. Neither had any information been offered. It was clear that the men didn't want to disclose their names or reveal where they lived. They were poachers and had broken the law. They were helping her but that was about it.

Screened by the canopy, sunlight broke through only in clearings. But openings were rare. Trees stood erect everywhere—like an army of soldiers. Chitra felt that she was passing through endless ranks of them. Several of the silent soldiers had fallen and sometimes, where a giant had toppled, neighbouring comrades had been dragged down too.

Their passage through the forest was fast and furious. Leaves crackled and thundered under their feet. Worried by the intensity of sound, Chitra kept glancing over her shoulder, keeping a lookout for her pursuers. Her companions constantly scanned the forest too. Chitra suspected she knew why. There were Jarawa here. The land they were passing through belonged to the dark-skinned original inhabitants of the Andaman Islands. They were intruding in their territory. An encounter could be dangerous.

Luckily for them the forest sprang no surprises. All they heard was birds and the scurrying of lizards under the leaf carpet. They encountered no animals, except once, when Chitra spotted a huge monitor lizard. After staring at them and flicking a forked tongue in their direction it dashed off into the undergrowth. The lines of the animal were so dinosaur-like that Chitra was convinced the monitor was a leftover from prehistoric times.

It was an hour or more, estimated Chitra, before the men finally pulled up. Water bottles were passed around once again. This time, after they had gulped their share, the bottles were drained. Were the men close to their destination, wondered Chitra? It was either that or there was a waterhole ahead.

The man with the thin face turned to Chitra. 'If you go straight down from here you will come to the creek,' he said. 'You will see mangrove before you reach the creek. Turn right there, and if you keep going you will come to their camp.'

'Straight and right before the creek,' repeated Chitra.

The man nodded, his eyes pearly-white against his dark skin.

Chitra smiled. 'Thank you for all your help. You saved my life, I will always be grateful for that.' She paused a moment and then continued, 'I don't even know who you are.'

'It is better we keep it that way, madam.'

'Fine,' replied Chitra. 'But I want to tell you my name. I am Chitra Shankaran.'

'I know you are Shankaran madam. I have seen you before with your father at Rangat bus stop.'

Chitra's mouth popped open. She stared at the man in undisguised surprise.

'Your father has come before to our village, and my friends have helped him find swiftlet caves. Your father would have been angry if he saw what we did today.'

'Yes, he would have been angry,' agreed Chitra. 'Very angry. But he would not have gone to the police as you might expect. He would have talked to you instead.'

'We need money,' said the thin-faced man, looking into Chitra's eyes. 'No sensible person comes to Jarawa territory. We took the risk today. We need money for our sister's marriage.'

Chitra kept silent. She couldn't pass off what they had done simply because their sister was getting married.

The man seemed to hesitate, then he spoke. 'The men chasing you are bad. Nobody goes to their camp, it is dangerous. You can come with us if you want. Our village is only two hours from here, and the Andaman Trunk Road passes through it.'

Chitra smiled and shook her head. 'Thank you,' she said sincerely. 'I appreciate your offer, but I cannot leave my friends.'

Chitra held out her hand and the men shook it one by one. 'I will never forget your help,' she called after them as they departed.

The men waved and Chitra waved back.

The forest quickly swallowed the men, and soon Chitra was alone; just her and the birds. Turning, she set out in the direction they had instructed.

THE HIDEOUT

Chitra quickly discovered that steering a straight path through a healthy, undisturbed forest wasn't easy. Fallen trees, tall ones in particular, forced her to deviate long distances. Even the standing giants of the forest impeded her progress. Many possessed trunks that were broader than the side of a truck. And in addition to mammoth-sized trunks there were roots to contend with. Enormous buttress roots snaked everywhere, unfurling like fences across the forest floor. The accompanying underbrush didn't make matters any easier, and a doubtful, general direction was the best Chitra could maintain.

Chitra hurried along as fast as she could. Time was of the essence. Her pursuers would have reported their failure by now, and there was every possibility that Patrick might already have shifted base in response.

It wasn't long before the texture of the soil began to change beneath Chitra's feet, turning sticky. Soon, the forest giants fell behind, and she was confronted by a tangle of mangrove. Through their pencil-like trunks a ribbon of light was visible. It was the creek all right, but in-between stretched acres of slush.

Chitra had no intention of entering the swamp. She had been instructed to turn right at the creek. Switching direction, she skirted along the edge of the swamp.

Chitra smelled woodsmoke long before she saw the camp. She eased her gait, treading cautiously now. Yet, in spite of her light footfalls, the carpet of leaves made silent progress impossible. Fearing detection, she entered the soft, oozy mud of the swamp. Chitra grimaced as sticky slime cloaked her again. But her passage was soundless now, and the knotted mangrove roots offered excellent cover. Preferring water over slush, Chitra waded deeper into the swamp, till she was hip-deep and could choose between swimming and walking.

The smoke issued from a cooking fire. Chitra spotted it through a screen of roots. She swam slowly round the roots with just her nose and eyes out of the water. There was a wooden platform at the edge of the mangrove swamp. Two men were sitting on the platform on bamboo stools and a game of cards was in progress. Chitra identified the men instantly—the pair that had been pursuing her.

The fire burned some distance from the platform, on a raised mound. There was a stove above the flames with vessels balanced on it. A man with a gun slung across his shoulders squatted nearby, cutting vegetables.

Behind the platform Chitra saw two crude, roofed shelters. A man sat in one of the shelters, leafing through a magazine. In the other shelter sat Vikram and Alex. Chitra breathed a sigh of relief on seeing her friends. They were alive and well. They looked comfortable, despite the fact that they were bound hand-and-foot. There was no sign of Aditya, however.

Chitra inspected the forest on either side of the camp, looking for Aditya. In the water there was a scaffolding-like structure. The structure gleamed where it caught the sun, indicating it was made of metal. Chitra counted eight posts arranged in pairs. The lead pair stood in deep water while the others behind led to land, the last two standing on solid ground. Each of the pairs was connected by a cross member, so that the entire structure looked like a tunnel that led from water to dry land. A large hut with a bolted door stood behind the metal posts.

Chitra stared at the scaffolding. There was a dungi floating beneath it and a massive hook dangled from the crossbeams. It was the hook that provided Chitra a clue, enabling her to identify the structure for what it was. She had seen similar metallic contraptions at ports. The tunnel-like structure was a crane. Though a miniature version of the monstrous cranes at Port Blair, it was large enough to unload cargo from dungis. The hut behind the crane had to be a storage shed—a godown.

A set of roofs, similar to the ones sheltering the platforms, covered the crane and storage shed. Someone had invested considerable time and effort in screening the camp from the air. Was this some kind of a smuggling operation, wondered Chitra? Everything she had seen at the camp seemed to indicate so. Something was being stored at this carefully hidden hideout. Something Patrick was willing to kill for to protect its secrecy.

Chitra continued her search for Aditya, probing the area around the crane and the shed. Flicking her gaze across the swamp, she spotted a small rubber boat floating near the crane. It was their Gemini dinghy.

A channel of water snaked forward past the Gemini, twisting between half-submerged mangrove trees. Chitra's eyes followed the channel to where the trees thinned, and the creek shone through a veil of leaves and branches.

A splash-like sound disturbed Chitra, and she saw a fish leap from the water. It flashed silver in the sunlight before falling back into the green soup of the swamp. The presence of the fish jolted Chitra, sending a shiver through her: she was in crocodile territory. It struck her that it was daytime now. Her torch would not protect her. Tension knotted Chitra's stomach. The swamp waters were dangerous.

As Chitra stood undecided, wondering whether to seek the safety of land, she heard the sound of an engine. The men at the camp had obviously heard it too, but they showed no concern. The armed cook hunched beside his fire, the game of cards proceeded undisturbed, and the man in the shelter continued to read. Vikram and Alex seemed to be the only ones paying attention to the sound. Chitra saw their lips move as they exchanged words inaudible to her.

Chitra waited. The rhythmic chugging grew louder, and a shadow appeared on the glittering waters of the creek. The swamp turned silent when the engine of the boat was cut. Chitra heard the wash of waves followed by the slap of paddles. The water was shallow, and the boat was being poled forward.

Chitra lost sight of the boat as it disappeared behind a thicket of mangrove. When she spotted it next it was closer, emerging from behind a screen of roots and trees. The boat was a dungi. Two men stood fore and aft with poles in their hands. Two more sat in-between, working paddles. Patrick stood at the prow, steering the vessel with his pole.

As the dungi drew near it dropped speed, and to Chitra's surprise, it halted. Patrick was leaning on his pole and speaking. Straining her ears, Chitra faintly picked out his voice. He was addressing somebody or something in a clump of mangrove trees opposite him. It was when Chitra looked at the trees that she saw Aditya.

Chitra's breath caught in her throat. Aditya was standing in knee-deep water. He was bound to a tree, arms stretched back along its trunk and lashed behind him. He was facing the creek, and all she could see of him was a side profile.

The shock of seeing her friend tied so helplessly in the water lifted as quickly as it came. His punishment—Chitra was convinced he had been punished—seemed to have had little effect on him. There was a grin on Aditya's face, and she heard him shout a cheery reply to Patrick. Aditya must have behaved intolerably to drive his captors to banish him to the swamp. Chitra smiled inwardly, wondering what extreme stunt he had pulled on them.

The men in the boat were laughing, and Aditya shouted once more at them. They laughed even louder as they leaned on their poles, propelling their dungi forward.

Chitra's breath caught once more as she stared at Aditya. There was no one guarding him! He could be set free without alerting his captors!

Chitra stared excitedly at the water. Possibly a hundred metres of swamp lay between her and Aditya. The wall of mangrove that shielded her from the camp would allow her to cover half the distance without danger. But ahead lay the open waterway. To get to Aditya she would have to hazard swimming across it.

The swamp resounded with laughter and talk. The men in the dungi were hailing their friends on shore. Her pursuers had risen from their chairs. The cook had joined them, and the man who had been reading was crossing to their platform.

Chitra swam quickly towards deeper water. The men would be occupied for a while exchanging greetings. This was a good time to attempt the crossing. She kept her head down, skirting around roots and ducking behind trees. Crocodiles posed a threat as dangerous as Patrick and his men, and she kept a lookout for ripples and shadows on the water. Thankfully, no crocodiles bothered her. Reaching the waterway, she paused at its edge.

The waterway wasn't entirely open. Mud-banks protruded like tiny islands along its length and irrepressible mangrove trees poked at random from its murky waters. But the cover wasn't dense enough to screen surface movements—she would have to swim underwater.

Chitra looked at the camp.

The dungi had anchored beside the central platform and its occupants had disembarked. There had been four men at the camp earlier and an additional five had arrived on the dungi. Chitra counted nine men—all were gathered on the main platform.

Chitra aerated her lungs. Targeting a tree midway across the waterway, she drew a deep breath and submerged herself. A green world, bright and awash with tiny particles, surrounded her. Yet, in spite of the brightness, visibility was poor, and Chitra wondered how crocodiles could see in this underwater realm of theirs. She stayed as low as possible, her chest inches above the mud. She swam with restrained strokes, curbing kicks and lunges that might disturb the surface. She quickly discovered that swimming in a straight line to her chosen tree was impossible. She was forced to twist and weave, bumping and scraping against roots and dark unidentifiable objects. Chitra swam far, till she was confronted by a web of roots that blocked forward movement.

She broke surface, but for only a moment, and generating barely a ripple, submerged herself once more. Chitra swam blindly, concentrating only on dodging obstacles that materialised from the gloom, surfacing finally when her protesting lungs forced her to. With just her nose and eyes out of the water, she peered at the camp.

The men were chatting on shore. Her crossing had gone unnoticed. Aditya wasn't far now; she could see him clearly. Chitra smiled when she gazed at him. Aditya was sleeping. His eyes were shut, and his head had rolled to one side. Only Aditya could have dozed off in such an uncomfortable position—standing, with his arms stretched and lashed behind.

Slithering across the mud, Chitra slowly made her way towards him. Aditya's eyes were still closed when Chitra halted beneath his tree.

For the first time that day Chitra felt conscious of her appearance. Her hair was cloaked with slime. Her face was unwashed and mud-crusted, and her clothes were soggy and filthy. Her only consolation was that Aditya looked an equal mess.

A mischievous gleam twinkled in Chitra's eyes. Raising her hand, she made a splashing sound in the water.

The effect on Aditya was comical.

His body jerked violently and his legs shot out from under him. Chitra held back a giggle as she saw his face contort with fear, his eyes almost popping from their sockets. Then he saw her, and his expression changed from outright terror to a mixture of relief and anger.

'*You!*' he breathed in a strangled voice. Chitra stared up at him through laughing eyes.

'You . . . you . . . you scared me,' stuttered Aditya. 'What did you have to do that for? Is this some kind of a girlie prank? I thought you were a crocodile!'

Chitra placed a hand on her mouth, muffling her laughter.

'Just you wait,' gasped Aditya. 'I'll get even with you.'

Chitra continued to laugh silently.

As the shock subsided, so did Aditya's anger, and a rueful grin appeared on his face as he saw the funny side of Chitra's prank.

Aditya looked down at Chitra, sighing. 'Your return is going to cost me. Alex and I had a bet. He was convinced that you'd get away. I didn't agree with him.'

Chitra snorted. 'No confidence because I'm a woman, huh? You men are all alike. Can't admit that a woman can do better than you. Typical MCP attitude.'

'MC is right,' smirked Aditya. 'Most men are chauvinists.'

'You are a PIG, Aditya Khan, you left out the pig in MCP.'

Aditya exhaled wearily. 'A pig if you say so, Chitra. At this moment I accept whatever you say. I'm so glad to have you back.'

'Wow!' exclaimed Chitra, looking impressed. 'A reformed male. Maybe there is hope for us worthless women. But what mischief have you been up to?' Her eyes twinkled. 'Why have they tied you here?'

'They were upset with me.'

'They would be, to abandon you to the crocs.'

'I called them names. I guess they didn't like that.'

'Is that all?' asked Chitra.

'Not quite. I must have angered them when I attacked the men who came to feed us this morning. I had knocked one down and I would have escaped if the second man, a hulk called Anand, wasn't so strong. We were grappling in the mud and his yells brought the rest of them along. The man I knocked down was angry. It was he who insisted that they tie me up in the middle of the swamp as crocodile meat. The water has gone down now, but when they left me here, I was chest-deep in the muck. It was scary for a while, but no crocs came along till you arrived pretending to be one.'

Chitra had extracted her penknife from her pouch while he talked.

'Careful,' said Aditya, as Chitra grasped roots and lifted herself from the mud. 'Don't let them see you.'

'They can't,' grunted Chitra. 'I'm shielded by the trunk of your tree.'

Chitra pressed her feet deep into the slush as she rose. Standing in the squelchy slime was difficult, and she had to hold on to Aditya to steady herself.

'Wonder Woman to the rescue,' whispered Aditya, as Chitra stood level with him, matching his six-foot height.

Chitra flicked her knife under his nose. 'No cracks,' she warned.

'Sorry, madam!' apologised Aditya. 'Will you be so kind as to cut my ropes?'

'That's better,' said Chitra, leaning across him. 'I like it when you speak that way.'

Aditya sniffed. His nose was buried in Chitra's mud-crusted hair. 'You smell terrible,' he said, unable to resist the quip.

Chitra jabbed her blade against his palm.

'Ouch!' exclaimed Aditya.

'I warned you, didn't I?' said Chitra. 'Now. Shall we be polite again?'

'Yes, madam,' said Aditya in a meek voice. 'Please cut my bonds, madam. Your assistance will relieve the terrible ache in my shoulders and immensely improve my blood circulation. I can't wait to lower my hands.'

'Uh-huh,' said Chitra, working her knife. 'Don't even think of lowering your arms just now. The men at the camp might notice.'

Aditya cried with relief as the bonds fell away. His captors had been ruthless when they had trussed him up, stretching his arms as far back as possible. The constricting posture had set off cramps. Aditya had been silently bearing the pain since.

Chitra sank back into the mud.

While Aditya, eyes screwed tight, waited for circulation to return to his shoulders, she peeped through the vegetation, looking back at the camp. Aditya's release had gone unnoticed. Yet Chitra wasn't prepared to take any risks. He would have to keep his arms up and wrapped around the tree no matter how much it hurt him.

'Feeling better?' asked Chitra, after a while.

Aditya replied through gritted teeth. 'If you call the sensation of boiling oil squirting through your shoulder joints pleasurable, I'm fine. Can't I lower my arms for a minute at least?'

The suffering on Aditya's face melted Chitra's resolve. Maybe he could if no one was watching. She glanced at the camp and her face turned white, blood draining from it.

'Don't move!' she gasped. 'Someone's headed this way.'

'Oh no!' groaned Aditya.

'Maybe he isn't . . . no he is . . . he's stepped into the swamp. He's wading this way with something in his hands . . . I think it's a tiffin-box.'

'They haven't fed me at all. Hell! What a time for them to take pity on me.'

'He'll be here in a couple of minutes!' cried Chitra. 'What do I do?'

'Can you tie the rope back?'

'No, he'll see me.'

'We'll have to run for it,' said Aditya.

'No, wait . . . the Gemini. The man is still far away. Stay here, Aditya, I'll swim and get the dinghy.'

'But—'

'Don't argue!' hissed Chitra. 'I'm fed up with the forest and running all day. With the Gemini we can escape down the creek. We can get away once and for all! I'll be back with the dinghy. You handle the man, he's small and thin.'

Chitra threw herself into the mud before Aditya could respond. Scrabbling on all fours, she worked her way to deeper water. When it rose to her hips she submerged herself and swam towards the waterway. Soon, her breath ran out and she surfaced, checking her bearings.

She had reached the waterway.

The Gemini floated upstream of her.

Immersing herself once more, she swam as far upstream as her lungs allowed. The Gemini bobbed just a short distance ahead, and Chitra, aware she was running out of time, submerged herself again.

The water was shallow where the Gemini was moored, and Chitra half swam, half pulled herself along the final stretch. She located the anchor rope and yanked hard on it. The rope had been loosely tied, and her energetic tug dislodged it from the foliage. Chitra swam to the nose of the dinghy, not bothering to submerge herself. Time was running out; she was sacrificing stealth for speed. Grabbing the circular hook at the nose, she treaded water, pulling the dinghy behind her. Chitra was acutely aware that the dinghy was visible from the camp and that its forward displacement could be spotted any moment.

Aditya had thought Chitra had gone crazy when she had flung herself into the mud. The Gemini plan made no sense to him. The dinghy was clearly visible from the camp, and shifting it was far too dangerous. He couldn't understand why they hadn't just run for the forest. But Chitra had gone before he could protest, and he was left clenching his fists in frustration.

Aditya had been tied facing the creek. The camp and the Gemini lay behind him. All the action was taking place beyond his field of vision. There was nothing he could do till either Chitra or the man arrived. The man . . . it suddenly struck Aditya that the man was approaching from behind. Would he notice that the rope binding his hands was missing? Before he began to panic, Aditya recollected that there was thick foliage behind him. There was little possibility of the missing rope being noticed.

Chitra could see the man with the tiffin from the waterway. But even as she looked, she gagged. There wasn't just one man, as she had seen earlier. Chitra stared in horror. A second man followed the tiffin-wallah. The newcomer was big and bulky, and he had a gun tucked in his belt.

If Chitra could, she would have smacked herself. What a fool she had been! It was obvious that they would send along an armed escort. Aditya's past behaviour justified the necessity. But in her haste, she hadn't considered the possibility.

The approaching men had forged ahead of Chitra and were closer to Aditya than she was. Though trees and foliage shielded her from them, she and the Gemini would instantly be spotted if either of them glanced her way. Chitra lowered herself, till like a crocodile, she swam with just her nose and eyes above the water. She was hidden . . . but the dinghy . . . it was only a matter of time before somebody spotted the drifting Gemini.

Aditya fumed silently at Chitra when he heard the sound of voices behind him. The possibility of a second man had occurred to him, but Chitra hadn't allowed him to reason with her. The men were chatting in Hindi, and from the snatches he heard, he gathered that both were unhappy with the task of wading out so deep into the swamp. One of the men was complaining loudly at the futility of coming all this way to feed him. What was the point, argued the man, especially since it had been decided to dispose of their captives? Why feed them if they were to be killed? The second man provided the answer. Patrick was holding back because of the escaped girl. The decision on the prisoners' fate would be taken only when Patrick was sure of what had become of her.

The first man wasn't convinced. Their chore was a waste of time according to him. He fretted continuously as they negotiated their way to where Aditya was tied. It was as the men drew level with him that Aditya heard a shout. He froze! Had they noticed his hands weren't bound? But it wasn't that.

'Look,' cried one of the men in Hindi. 'The dinghy—'

Chitra had been discovered.

Chitra heard the cry too and submerged herself.

'How could it have drifted so far?' wondered a puzzled voice.

'Who anchored it?' the other wanted to know.

'Wasn't me, it was John.'

Aditya couldn't remain a bystander anymore. The men were occupied with the dinghy. They were not looking at him. It was safe for him to move. Lowering his arms, he edged himself around the trunk. The men stood with their backs to him. The man holding the tiffin was the smaller of the two. Aditya recognised the second, bigger man. It was Anand, the brawny hulk he had wrestled earlier. There was a gun protruding from his belt.

Aditya grimaced with pain as he lowered his arms. They were stiff and unimaginably heavy. He was in no condition for a tussle, especially with two men. He stood no chance against them. But the weapon provided a ray of hope. If only he could appropriate Anand's gun.

'There's something below the dinghy,' said the man with the tiffin.

'Yes . . . the water is moving,' said Anand.

A pool of slush separated Aditya from the men.

'A fish—?' the man with the tiffin wondered aloud.

Moving carefully, Aditya placed a foot in the slush pool.

'It's too long for a fish . . . maybe a crocodile?'

Balancing in the mud, Aditya advanced another step.

Out on the waterway, the dinghy rocked as Chitra struggled to hold her breath beneath it.

'What could it—' But Anand did not complete his sentence. A faint squelching prompted him to turn.

Aditya was standing right behind Anand.

As the man swung around Aditya reached for his waist and grasping the butt of his gun, plucked it from his belt. Following up swiftly, Aditya lowered his shoulder and smashed it into Anand with all the force he could muster. Aditya was a heavy boy and Anand, unbalanced at that moment, toppled into the mud.

'Don't move!' hissed Aditya, turning the gun on the man with the tiffin who looked thunderstruck. 'Neither of you move or speak,' he warned, swinging the weapon between the tiffin-wallah and the mud-splattered Anand, who was struggling to rise. 'Move and I shoot!' snarled Aditya. There was a desperate ring of conviction in his voice, and it must have carried enough meaning, because Anand made no further attempt to rise.

Chitra surfaced beside the dinghy and stared in astonishment at what she saw.

'Keep pulling the dinghy,' called out Aditya, watching her from the corner of his eye.

Chitra grasped the lead rope of the Gemini and swam forward, tugging furiously.

Aditya looked across at the camp. The men were busy with their meal. They hadn't noticed anything amiss as yet, but if they happened to glance in their direction, they certainly would. Vikram and Alex, however, were staring at him. Aditya raised a clenched fist for them before returning his gaze to his captives.

'Give me the tiffin,' ordered Aditya, remembering he was hungry. 'Leave it on the ground,' he instructed, 'and back away.' The man did as bid and Aditya, balancing in the mud, plucked it from the ground.

Though still in the waterway, Chitra was level with him now, and she had pulled herself into the dinghy. She was crouched beside the engine, tinkering with its controls. 'Come on,' she called, her voice low. 'Let's leave!'

Aditya backed away from the men, his gun covering them.

A screen of trees and foliage was coming up between Aditya and the men as he waded towards the Gemini.

'There's going to be trouble,' warned Chitra. 'You won't be able to keep them in control; they're going to shout for help.'

There was little Aditya could do. The men were bound to start yelling the moment his gun no longer covered them.

Anticipating the worst, Chitra crouched beside the motor, starter rope in hand.

Aditya was still a considerable distance from Chitra when the men began to shout. Chitra jerked the engine cord. The motor turned but did not start. She heard answering calls from the camp as she fiddled with the choke and pulled the cord again. This time the motor roared to life and Chitra twisted the throttle, accelerating the boat towards Aditya.

Aditya tossed the tiffin-box and gun into the boat and leapt in. Chitra turned the dinghy towards the waterway. Finding a clear section, she opened the throttle wide.

The Gemini surged forward.

Gunfire rang out from the camp, and Chitra started as a deafening sound exploded beside her. She turned and saw Aditya grinning at her, smoking gun in hand. His gun exploded again and again as he pulled the trigger.

An island of trees and brush came up between the camp and the dinghy, and Chitra banked tightly around it. The camp was screened off and Aditya, surmising he would be wasting his limited supply of bullets, stopped firing.

Gunshots continued to ring out behind them, but the intervening foliage absorbed the bullets. Ahead, the waterway widened, and soon they were in the creek.

ON THE WATER

Chitra yelled in triumph.

Aditya whooped and punched the air with delight.

Above them, blue skies replaced the canopy. The oppressive forest retreated to the creek banks, and a breeze refreshed their sweaty brows.

An engine motor roared to life behind them.

'There's no need to worry,' shouted Chitra. 'They can't catch us. The Gemini is much too fast for their dungis.'

'What about fuel?' asked Aditya. 'How far can we go?'

'There isn't much,' admitted Chitra, examining the tank at her feet. 'But there's some in Alex's dungi. We'll stop there and refuel. After that it's a three-hour run for Mayabunder. Once there we can alert the police and the navy. If we can convince the navy, they'll have helicopters here before dark to rescue Vikram and Alex.'

'Helicopters?' goggled Aditya.

'There are no roads here. Copters are the only way to get here in a hurry. If they don't come quickly, Patrick and his men will be gone.'

Chitra's spirits were high.

This was the way to travel! The creek was a four-lane expressway compared to the vegetation-choked forest. It stretched forward like a silken highway, not a ripple on its surface. The Gemini shredded its mirror-still coat, spewing eddies and currents in its wake.

'HANG ON!' shouted Chitra.

Aditya grasped a tie-rope as Chitra took a bend at high speed. Her excitement was infectious, and Aditya experienced an exuberant tingle in his veins. The power of the engine, the racy response of the dinghy, the feel of the wind—all blended in a heady mix. Aditya wished it was he who had the throttle in his hands.

Flashing round a bend they disturbed a flock of brown birds with long curved bills. Flapping their wings in alarm, they flew low above the water, disappearing around the next curve.

They spotted the birds once more when Chitra gunned the boat about the bend.

'Whimbrels,' shouted Chitra.

The birds had settled on a mud bank. As the dinghy sped towards them, they launched themselves in the air once more. The birds accompanied them throughout their creek journey, flying fast and staying ahead of the dinghy. They rested often, on the trees or along the muddy shore, only to wing their way forward every time they were disturbed.

Aditya was envious of the skill Chitra displayed with the dinghy. He contemplated asking her to hand him the throttle, but guessing she wouldn't, he dropped the idea.

He occupied himself instead with the tiffin-box, ravenously attacking the soggy chapatis and muddy vegetables he found inside.

Chitra accepted only one chapati. 'Finish the rest,' she shouted. 'I've eaten earlier.'

The creek snaked endlessly forward. On one of the numerous mudbanks they spotted a pair of crocodiles hurriedly submerging as they hurtled past. The mysterious shadows of the night were gone, supplanted by an exuberance of green. The shores were packed solid with mangrove. Behind, soared the taller forest trees. The creek waters were a mirror. Like a picture-perfect painting, they reflected the lush vegetation on either bank. Aditya lost count of the bends in the creek and the number of times they propelled the whimbrels into flight. Finally, with the whimbrels leading the way, they hit the wide waters of Lewis Inlet.

Aditya looked at Chitra as she turned the dinghy, guiding it to the open sea. Mud-streaks stained her windswept hair. Though unwashed, her face glowed red and healthy and her eyes sparkled as if she was enjoying every moment of their flight. 'Wild' was the word that sprang to Aditya's lips. This girl was no pretender. She was a genuine outdoorswoman, probably better equipped with survival skills than he. In size as well as ability, he had met his match in Chitra.

Presently, they reached an open section of water. Itching for the throttle, Aditya thought it safe enough to take over the controls. Tapping Chitra's shoulder he requested her for the throttle. Chitra looked blankly at him for a moment, then shrugging, she moved aside. Aditya grabbed the lever. Turning it slowly, he gradually built up speed till the dinghy was leaping the waves from crest to crest.

'Keep the nose pointed to the waves,' instructed Chitra, as the water grew choppy. 'Take a left for Alex's boat when we hit the sea. Be careful, there are rocks there. Give them a wide berth.'

Chitra didn't like the feel of the wind as they neared the sea. It was blowing strong and there were whitecaps on the water. Mayabunder lay to their right, but Alex's boat was beached on their left. Landing and collecting fuel would consume precious minutes. Then they would have to double back across the inlet for Mayabunder. They had won themselves a good lead, but Chitra wondered whether it would be enough.

She turned to Aditya. 'Give me the controls. The sea is rough, we might lose time.'

'I can handle it,' replied Aditya shortly.

'Sure, you can. But I have more experience. We have to double back after collecting the fuel. Speed is essential.'

'You're not the only one who can go fast.' Aditya flashed his eyes. 'Watch me!'

Chitra couldn't believe her ears. This wasn't the time for childish behaviour. Their lives and that of their friends were at stake. She stared incredulously but Aditya refused to look at her.

The dinghy was moving out of the inlet into the open sea, and the rocks Chitra had spoken of had come up on their left. Aditya's attention was riveted on the furthest rock, where he would have to turn the boat. White terns, pearly in the sunlight, pranced on the rocks. Waves surged and foamed against them, and crabs scuttled about their surface, somehow avoiding the fury of the lashing waves.

The sea was rough. Aditya would have to judge his turn carefully. But Aditya's confidence was high, and the dinghy leapt forward as he gunned the engine.

'Careful,' warned Chitra.

Aditya did not reply.

The rocks flashed by and when he passed the last one, Aditya thrust hard at the rudder.

'Wide turn,' shouted Chitra. 'Not so sharp!'

But her cries were too late. Aditya had turned too abruptly. A frothing mountain of water exploded over the dinghy, flooding it and drenching both teenagers. The tiffin-box bobbed and vanished over the edge.

'Keep going!' screamed Chitra. 'Don't let the throttle go!'

Aditya hung on, twisting hard on the throttle. The dinghy responded slowly, rising sluggishly above the waves. It gradually gathered speed, but the damage had been done. Its floorboards were awash with water.

'Head for the beach!' instructed Chitra. 'There's Alex's dungi.'

Aditya guided the rubber boat, pointing its nose at the tiny strip of beach. But the dinghy was carrying the additional weight of water, and it moved at a perceptibly slower speed.

'Ride the waves,' shouted Chitra. 'Hold the nose steady!'

The dinghy ploughed through the waves, and when Aditya was sure that the tide would carry him in, he cut the engine, allowing the surf to complete the journey for them.

Chitra was up and out in a flash. 'Look after the Gemini,' she called, as she sprinted across wet sand to Alex's dungi.

A tern, perched on the dungi's prow, squawked and took wing as Chitra approached. Alex stored his fuel in jerrycans placed in the mid-section of the boat. Chitra searched but didn't find them. Except for a few plastic water bottles there was nothing in the boat—the dungi had been stripped clean.

Chitra stared in horror. Somebody—possibly their captors themselves—had raided the boat. All the extra fuel had been taken.

Aditya shouted from the shore. 'Don't stand there. Hurry! Get the fuel!'

'There is no fuel. It's stolen, gone!'

'What?'

Chitra stood dumbstruck, gazing at the dungi.

'What are we waiting for then?' bellowed Aditya. 'Move and bring along anything that might be useful.'

Chitra rallied herself. She quickly collected the water bottles. There was an empty tin can in the well of the boat—a bailer. It would be useful for the water that had collected in the Gemini. Clutching her booty to her chest, she ran back to the dinghy.

Aditya was holding the Gemini in knee-deep water. Chitra splashed into the boat, and dumping her load she sprang for the motor.

'Point the nose to the waves,' she instructed.

Aditya turned the boat around, the sea foaming about his knees.

Crouching, Chitra yanked the starter.

The engine caught smoothly, and when Aditya leapt in, Chitra powered the dinghy. A large wave pounded towards them as she accelerated. Aditya clutched the water bottles and bailer as the Gemini met the wave head on. The force of the wave brought the boat to a halt, but it spiritedly climbed the frothy crest and rode down the other side, picking up speed once more. The next wave was tackled in a similar manner, and they soon crossed the surf-line, easing into the swells of the open sea.

Chitra turned the boat northwards, back towards Lewis Inlet. Her eyes scanned its waters, searching for the pursuing dungi.

'There's the dungi!' shouted Aditya.

Chitra spotted it. Patrick's green boat was exiting the inlet, near the rocks. Chitra turned the Gemini round, tracing a wide circle. Their route to Mayabunder had been cut off.

'Bail the water!' she shouted at Aditya. 'We have to rid ourselves of all unnecessary weight to stay ahead.'

Aditya bent to his task, tin can in hand.

The dungi could not catch them. Of that Chitra was sure, but fuel was a problem. Their supply was limited to a few inches of liquid—less than an hour's supply. The nearest settlement in the southerly direction they were headed was Uttara Jetty. But there was no hope of reaching Uttara. Their fuel would run out less than halfway there. Ditching the dinghy was a certainty.

Aditya stared aft as he bailed. 'They've crossed the rocks. They're turning, coming after us.'

'They can't catch us,' Chitra assured him. 'But we're going to have to abandon our dinghy when the fuel runs out.'

Aditya paused from his task. 'How much time do we have?'

'Less than an hour.'

'Does that mean Jarawa territory?'

Chitra nodded. 'I'm afraid so.'

Aditya's cheeks creased in a smile. 'So, we are going to meet the Jarawa after all.'

Chitra sighed. 'Who knows? Let's not bother about them for now. There's enough on our hands.'

The beach to their left had been replaced by rock and an unbroken line of trees, stretching as far as the eye could see. The forest was dark and empty. If there were any Jarawa here, they weren't advertising their presence. The only sign of life was the dungi behind and a large sea eagle hovering above.

Neither Chitra nor Aditya spoke. Chitra was still annoyed with Aditya for not handing back the controls. Aditya, on his part, worked tirelessly at bailing, battling the wind-tossed sea that sloshed water in by the bucketful.

It was a beautiful afternoon. The sky was deep blue and clear, except for a scattering of silver-white clouds near the horizon. The sea heaved and rolled, reflecting flashes of sunlight. If only she could draw a mental screen, wished Chitra; if she could shut out the dungi that clung wolf-like to their tail. The journey might actually have been pleasurable then—one of those typical lazy sea journeys, with the wind in her face and a magnificent coastline unfolding its beaches, promontories and grand forests. But this was no typical sea journey. It could end at any moment. And when it did, Aditya and she faced the unsettling prospect of a chase through a jungle wilderness that belonged to an unpredictable and fearsome people.

Though Chitra kept the throttle fully open, the Gemini seemed to be making no headway on the pursuing dungi. Despite the greater speed of the Gemini, the distance between the boats remained constant. It could only be the waves, speculated Chitra. Being smaller, the Gemini had to work its way through the waves, whereas the longer dungi, designed for the swells of the open sea, rode them with far more ease.

After an uneventful half-hour, while travelling a rocky shoreline, the motor jerked and abruptly cut off.

'Oh no!' breathed Chitra.

The motor couldn't have picked a worse spot to die. There were rocks in the water, and the sea was flecked white where waves broke against them. The rocks, in fact, had forced them further out to sea. The stretch of water to the shore was too long to swim; they wouldn't be able to cover it before the dungi arrived.

Reaching down, Chitra yanked desperately at the starter. The motor spun without catching. Crouching, she pulled several times, but the motor refused to start.

'Aditya,' panted Chitra. 'Raise the fuel tank, hold it above the motor.'

Balancing on the pitching floorboards, Aditya grasped the tank and held it at his waist. He inverted it so that whatever fuel remained trickled down the pipe. The motor coughed when Chitra yanked the starter and after a few tries it started.

'Don't let go of the tank, hold it up,' instructed Chitra. She turned the throttle only halfway, not daring to open it any further.

Aditya shook the tank and felt sloshing within. 'There is some fuel . . . but not much.'

'It has to hold till we cross the promontory ahead,' said Chitra. 'There is no place to land here. We have to find an area free of rocks.'

Aditya braced himself, balancing against the pitch of the dinghy. He turned every now and then, alternating his gaze between the dungi behind and the headland ahead. Their brief halt had enabled the dungi to cut the distance between them, and as Chitra nursed the Gemini along at only half-speed, the long boat steadily narrowed their lead.

Black rocks spiked out of the sea, forcing Chitra even further from the shore. Somewhere near the tip of the headland, the engine coughed and seized once more. The dungi drew inexorably closer as Chitra pulled away at the starter. Precious seconds ticked away. Aditya was beginning to consider abandoning the Gemini when the motor sputtered once more.

The motor held as they negotiated the rocks about the headland, and with racing hearts they stared at the shoreline unfolding around the bend. Black rocks retreated, yielding to a strip of golden sand. But Chitra's cry of relief froze in

her throat. The beach wasn't empty—a swarm of naked black figures thronged its golden sands.

'Jarawa,' she whispered, staring at the beach.

Several coal-black bodies stood in a row on the shore. These were not the effusive, dancing Jarawa that her father had seen. The group was mixed, comprising adults, teenagers and children too. But young or old, it mattered not—all held bows, with arrows pulled back, targeting them.

The motor died once more and this time neither Chitra nor Aditya bothered to restart it. The pursuing dungi was forgotten as they stared at the Jarawa.

'Don't seem very friendly, do they?' asked Aditya softly. Chitra did not reply. Her throat had gone dry.

The Jarawa stood still, like hunters watching their prey. Their arrows pointed unwaveringly at the teenagers. The tiny arrows the children held would not make it to the boat, but those the adults clasped surely would. Their attitude was unmistakably hostile. A careless or rash move was all it would take, and arrows would come flying their way.

'Laugh,' whispered Aditya, his face breaking into a broad grin. 'Giggle, look friendly.'

Though not feeling even remotely cheerful, Chitra smiled, and raising her hands, waved.

There was no answering smile or softening on the part of the Jarawa. Their arrows bristled steadfastly at them.

'Why don't they smile?' asked Chitra in a strangled voice, her beaming face masking her uneasiness.

'Your charm isn't working on them, Chitra. Lay it on thick. Stand up and wave.'

'Remind me to smack you, Aditya,' retorted Chitra. But she rose and contorting her face, laughed loudly.

A conference had begun. Two men were speaking, and another was shaking his head. The arrows did not waver.

'Whom do you prefer?' asked Aditya. Though he was grinning like a clown, his voice was serious. 'The Jarawa or our pursuers? We're going to have to make a choice soon.'

'Arrows or bullets?' asked Chitra, waving her hands. 'Is that it?'

'I prefer arrows,' said Aditya. 'I'm going to swim to the shore.' He glanced behind as he spoke.

The dungi had closed in considerably. A man was standing on its prow, a gun in his hand.

'Have you gone crazy?' exclaimed Chitra.

'They were good to your dad, remember?'

'But they were laughing then . . . dancing like this, see.' Chitra shook her body and undulated her arms.

'We'll have to take our chances,' said Aditya. 'I'm getting tired of holding this,' he complained, looking at the fuel tank he held. He bent to place it on the floorboard. The moment he hunched, one of the Jarawa drew his bowstring and released an arrow.

'WATCH OUT!' screamed Chitra, staring at the soaring arrow.

Aditya saw the arrow too.

Because of the distance, it had been launched skyward. Achieving its elevation, the arrow dipped and sped for the dinghy.

Since childhood, when he used to play with bows and toy arrows, Aditya had been confident that arrows could be

dodged. But as the Jarawa arrow descended, he discovered they couldn't. He was convinced that it was meant for him and a terror-stricken Chitra was certain it was coming for her. Both took evasive action, flinging themselves to the opposite ends of the dinghy. The arrow swooped downwards, smacking into the rubber bow of the dinghy. Air hissed noisily from the punctured bow as they stared dazedly at the quivering missile.

A gunshot exploded, warning them of the approaching dungi. The gun exploded a second time, and they heard the slap of a bullet against water.

Aditya scrambled to his feet. 'Jump!' he shouted. 'Swim for the shore!'

'But the Jarawa!' cried Chitra.

'They're gone, see!' Aditya pointed to the shore.

There was no one on shore. The beach had magically cleared.

Aditya grabbed Chitra by the hand and together they leapt into the water. Aditya kicked hard, breaking into a crawl. Chitra swam strongly beside him.

They were difficult targets, thought Aditya, as he battled the waves. Their horizontal bodies presented an awkward angle and besides, the marksman was sitting in a moving boat, shooting a handheld revolver. Aditya wasn't worried about getting hit, not for the moment, as the dungi was still some distance away. But Chitra and he had a long way to go for the shore. There was enough time for the boat to draw level with them. Up close they would be simple targets for the marksman.

But there was no turning back now. Aditya struck forward with all his strength. Chitra matched Aditya stroke for stroke and steadily pulled ahead of him. There was no time to raise their heads and sometimes, when they opened their mouths to breathe, water surged in, gagging them. Aditya swallowed water often. He felt he had gulped half the sea by the time he reached the surf-line.

With a swell gathering beneath him, Aditya raised his head, searching for the dungi behind. He spotted it near their abandoned Gemini. Surprisingly, it was no longer making for them. Instead, it was moving in a wide arc, away from the shore. The Burmese features of the marksman were clearly visible—it was Patrick. His gun arm was raised, and Aditya could hear repeated blasts as he fired. But the gun was not pointed at them; Patrick was shooting at the trees behind the beach and Aditya could see why. An arrow protruded from the shoulder of the man who sat beside the rudder. Patrick ducked as Aditya watched, and an arrow bounced off his dungi.

The Jarawa were shooting at their pursuers!

Another swell caught Aditya. A fizzing surge of foam swept him forward, and he found himself in hip-deep water.

Chitra was crouched in the bubbling sea waiting for him. She held out her hand and when he grasped it, she pulled him to her.

'What now?' she shouted in his ear.

'The forest,' he spluttered, holding on to her.

'But the Jarawa—'

'They aren't shooting at us. Look, they're targeting the dungi.'

Wiping salt and water from their eyes, Aditya and Chitra stared across the surf. The dungi was a long, dark log on the twinkling sea. It had turned and was drawing away from the shore.

Chitra looked at Aditya unconvinced. 'The Jarawa,' she repeated, 'They will shoot at us too.'

'But they're not. Don't you see! We are sitting targets for them. The Jarawa can pick us off if they want to. The men with the guns are their enemy!'

Aditya turned for the shore, but Chitra did not respond.

'Come on!' he implored, tugging her hand. 'Patrick will cut us down on the beach. We have to get to the cover of the forest, NOW!'

Aditya yanked Chitra, and holding her hand, he splashed forward. Emerging from the water they dashed across the narrow strip of beach, their feet flashing on burning sand. Chitra ran with the fear of an arrow piercing her heart while Aditya half-expected a bullet in his back. But their short dash was uneventful, and from the dazzle of the beach they entered the gloom of the forest.

THE JARAWA

Trees soared above them once more. Aditya blinked, adjusting his eyes to the sudden darkness about him. There were leaves on the ground and roots snaked everywhere. They heard a whistle followed by a shout. The calls were obviously directed at them. Refusing to heed the commands, Aditya kept running. But the whiz of an arrow followed by a solid 'thunk' as it hit the trunk of a tree brought them to a halt.

Chitra goggled at the arrow.

Leaves crackled and bushes quivered as feet thudded towards them.

Aditya grabbed Chitra's hand and squeezed. 'Smile,' he whispered.

Shadows were flitting in the forest. Without warning, as if materialising out of the air, a man appeared, black and completely naked. He held a bow with a drawn arrow. A large-nosed boy, possibly Aditya's age, emerged next and was followed by a group of silent children with round, white eyes. The boy and the children clutched bows and arrows too.

Aditya folded his hands as they approached. Chitra did the same, smiling broadly.

'Namaste,' said Chitra, bowing her head.

Aditya bowed and said 'namaste' too.

The children giggled, but a sharply spoken word from their elders silenced them.

The adult Jarawa was staring at them. A red thread girdled his waist, and another circled his neck like a fiery necklace. His face was thin, and his skin was darker than the night. His teeth flashed white as he opened his mouth and barked unintelligible words at Aditya. Detecting a questioning tone, Aditya interpreted his words as a query to their identity.

'Aditya,' he said, pointing to himself. Turning to Chitra, he spoke her name too.

The Jarawa shook his head. Pointing impatiently at the sea, he broke into a long monologue. Although they listened intently, Aditya and Chitra followed only one word, which the man repeated several times in his speech: 'Burma'.

'Burma,' said Chitra, nodding vigorously and pointing at the shimmering sea. 'Burma, badmaash,' she said. 'Burma badmaash,' she repeated, her eyes wide and expressive. She bunched her hand into a fist, except for two fingers which she pointed like a gun. She then turned the fingers on Aditya and herself and shouted, 'Bang, bang . . . Burma . . . badmaash . . . bang, bang.'

'Burma badmaash,' said the Jarawa slowly. 'Burma badmaash,' he repeated, looking at the girl with narrowed eyes.

Chitra nodded animatedly. 'Burma,' she said once more, and ran a finger across her throat. Then turning, she pretended to run, looking back over her shoulder.

The man lowered his bow and spoke rapidly to the thick-nosed boy beside him.

'Wow,' said Aditya, in a hushed tone. 'That was some performance.'

'It's working, I think,' breathed Chitra. 'Keep your fingers crossed. They don't like the Burmese. They hate it when Burmese poachers camp in their creeks.'

'Is that why they shot arrows at Patrick's dungi—because there were Burmese faces on board?' asked Aditya, whispering.

'Yes,' murmured Chitra. 'That's probably what saved us—the fact that we were running from people with Burmese faces.'

Aditya couldn't help noticing how lean and fit the Jarawa were. There wasn't an ounce of fat on their naked bodies and despite the absence of 'body-builder' type muscles, the man and the teenaged boy appeared robust and visibly strong. The children radiated well-being too, their tiny bodies dark and trim.

All of the Jarawa, including the children, had a cane bag strung behind them, held in place by a strap wrapped about their foreheads.

'There were more men, weren't there?' asked Chitra softly. She waved and winked at the children as she spoke. Smiling hesitantly, a little girl waved back.

'Yes,' replied Aditya in an undertone, sticking his tongue out at the kids. 'I think the others are in the trees near the beach making sure that the "Burma" people don't land.'

The conversation between the adult and the boy ended. The boy called softly. Then he turned and strode into the forest with the children following. Catching Aditya's eye, the man gestured that they follow.

Aditya and Chitra fell in step behind the children.

The children were strung in a line behind the Jarawa boy, with the little girl who had smiled at the rear. Chitra leaned forward and dipped her hand into the sling basket she carried.

'Fish,' she said, holding a small fish by the tail and showing it to Aditya.

'*Naapo*,' said the girl, turning her head.

'Naapo,' repeated Chitra, replacing the fish.

The girl nodded. Skipping to the boy in front of her she scooped something from the basket he carried. Turning, she placed it in Chitra's hand.

'Shell,' said Aditya.

'A bivalve,' corrected Chitra, staring at the twin-shelled mollusk she held. 'The flesh inside is edible. Our arrival must have interrupted a fishing trip. That's why these kids hold bows in their hands. The Jarawa fish with arrows in shallow water.'

The children crowded around Aditya and Chitra, proudly exhibiting their catch. They were smiling and eager, and they giggled and chattered as they dipped their hands in their baskets.

Chitra drew a sharp breath when she saw white, golf-ball like objects in one of the baskets. 'Turtle eggs,' she told Aditya, picking one.

'Ukkeela,' chorused the children, when Chitra handed an egg to Aditya. The egg was white and felt squashy soft in his hand.

But they were falling behind the teenaged boy, and the adult Jarawa barked terse words, at which the children scrambled back into line.

The forest was dark and cool. Enormous trees with tentacle-like branches shut out the overhead sun. One of the children began to sing in a high-pitched voice. Another joined in and soon all were belting out a rousing tune in perfect harmony.

'Le, ole, oh, le, ole, oh—'

It was a simple, cheerful chorus, and the teenaged boy in front and the man behind joined in. Chitra and Aditya sang along too. Chitra's voice was soft and melodious, but Aditya, who wasn't much of a singer, sang thoroughly off-key, drawing peals of laughter from the children.

It was a jolly procession that wound its way through the forest, and Aditya and Chitra felt their woes lift as they sang lustily with the Jarawa. After a cheery period of zestful marching, they crossed a stream. They came to a pond where they could smell wood-smoke. Around a bend they entered a clearing. There were four huts at its far end, simple ones, made of thatch resting on tall wooden logs. There were no doors or walls. Smoke rose from several logs scattered about the clearing, and a fire burned near one of the huts. The clearing swarmed with dark-skinned people. And like those that had intercepted them in the forest, they were entirely naked.

'Don't ogle,' Chitra warned Aditya, as the children ran gleefully into the clearing.

'And the same to you,' returned Aditya, surveying the Jarawa. 'Just look at them,' he continued admiringly. 'So well formed. No wonder they wear no clothes.'

Though one or two might have passed as plump, the majority of the Jarawa were well-proportioned and athletic. The entire community exuded health and youthfulness.

Aditya stared at the robust black bodies on display. 'I've never felt out of place with my clothes on. But here I feel distinctly so. Should we remove ours?'

Chitra turned red. 'Certainly not!' she snapped. 'I'm not going to, and don't you dare try removing yours.'

Their presence was causing a minor commotion. Activity in the clearing came to a halt as the Jarawa flocked forward to inspect them. Both Chitra and Aditya folded their palms and parroted the word 'namaste' as the Jarawa crowded about them, jabbering loudly. Neither had ever been the subject of such intense scrutiny and curiosity, and they handled it as best as they could, beaming at all who came to them. They sensed no hostility from the jostling crowd. There was much talking, laughing and merriment.

It was the girl whose cane bag Chitra had dipped her hand into who rescued them from the inquisitive crowd. She grabbed Chitra's wrist and tugged her away. Smiling at the adults, Chitra followed the child. Aditya, who had been waiting for such an opportunity, fell in behind them.

The girl led them to a corner of the clearing where a wood fire burned. The cane baskets the children had been carrying lay nearby, and an aluminium pan filled with water had been placed on rocks arranged about the fire. The girl sat beside the fire and Aditya and Chitra squatted next to her. The girl's face bubbled with delight as she reached for one of the baskets and emptied its contents—mussels—into the pan. A boy collected another basket and emptied it into the pan too.

'The adults aren't joining us,' observed Aditya, looking out across the fire at the Jarawa who were talking animatedly amongst themselves.

'They must be wondering what to do with us,' guessed Chitra. 'I hope they've accepted us.'

'I think they have,' said Aditya.

Chitra nodded. 'It seems so. Their attitude appears friendly. I don't fear them anymore.' She patted the little girl's head as she talked.

'Your Burma badmaash has worked wonders.'

Chitra grinned. 'Those Burmese faces were useful.'

'Probably saved our lives,' declared Aditya. 'That crowd of black bodies on the beach with arrows drawn is a sight I won't forget in a hurry. But what is a black race doing here? This is the Bay of Bengal. It isn't Africa, and if these people don't look African then I am a Martian.'

Chitra grinned. 'Look at their hair,' she said, patting the little girl's head. The girl's hair, like that of all the Jarawa, was short and tightly curled. 'This is typical Afro hair. I would have to pay a lot of money in a beauty salon for a hairstyle like hers.'

'So, they *are* African.'

Chitra shook her head. 'I didn't say that. Truth is no one actually knows. Their origin is still a mystery.'

'Oh, come on!' said Aditya. 'Of course, they are African. You gotta be dumb if you don't think so. Just look at them. They must have come across from Africa by boat.'

'Uh-huh,' said Chitra. 'There's plenty of proof that their race has been on these islands for several thousand years. But let's just assume one thousand years. Looking at them, do you think that these people had enough knowledge of the sea and possessed skills to build ocean-going vessels back then?'

Aditya shrugged. 'How would I know? But looking at them . . . they don't give me the feeling that they could have.'

'That is correct,' said Chitra. 'They didn't have the skills then, and fast forward to today, and even now the Jarawa don't know how to sail. They can't cross over to Sentinel Island, which is just thirty kilometres west of here. The sailing from Africa theory doesn't hold. There is a theory which claims that a boat carrying slaves from Africa was shipwrecked on these islands, and that these people are their descendants. There are plenty of other theories too, but the truth is that no one is sure of their origin—' Chitra broke off. The little girl was tugging at her hand.

'What's your name, sweetheart?' asked Chitra, turning to her.

The girl stared and then burst out laughing.

Chitra made a face. Holding the girl's shoulder, she pointed a finger at herself and said, 'Chitra'. She repeated the motion and pronounced her name once more. Then she turned her hand around, and pointing it at the girl, looked questioningly at her.

The girl's eyes twinkled as she replied. 'Meba,' she said.

'Meba,' repeated Chitra.

The girl nodded and pointing a finger at Chitra, said, 'Che-aah.'

Aditya's name was pronounced as, 'Adi-aah.'

The children giggled, repeating their names in a singsong manner, and Chitra and Aditya had to recite names like Leevpaa, Etto, Ab and Theenga. Chitra laughed and made faces at the children. But although Aditya smiled and mouthed names, his attention wandered across the clearing to the huts. There were bones and skulls hanging inside them that drew his curiosity.

'Those aren't human skulls,' laughed Chitra when Aditya pointed them out. 'They are wild boar skulls. Pigs are their favourite food, and they display the skulls as trophies.'

'Check out those plastic bottles,' said Aditya, pointing to the stacks of bottles inside the huts. The shiny bottles, some with Pepsi and Coca-Cola printed on them, seemed at odds with the primitive huts and naked tribals.

Chitra laughed. 'Soft drink companies would love that sight, wouldn't they? It's the ultimate advertisement for them—even the last of the primitive tribes enjoy our drinks! They could shoot an award-winning TV commercial here.'

Aditya chuckled. 'They'd have to censor the nudity, however. I wonder where they get their bottles from?'

'Could be from the villages and settlements at the edge of their reserve. The Jarawa go there often. Some might have been washed ashore too. Those net bags hanging from the poles are made from fishing nets that have been washed ashore. The aluminium vessels could be gifts presented to them by government contact parties.'

Aditya shook his head. 'I thought they were primitive people. Plastic bottles, net bags, cooking vessels . . . I didn't expect modern amenities here.'

'What did you expect?' asked Chitra, leaning forward and dipping her finger in the simmering vessel like some of the children were doing. The children giggled when she hurriedly withdrew her hand. She laughed with them before turning to Aditya. 'The Jarawa cannot escape us. We, the "civilized" people, are pressing on their reservation from all sides.'

'Twenty-first century tribals,' joked Aditya. 'These guys are certainly cool. Wonder when dark glasses and designer accessories will come along?'

'Don't knock them, Aditya. The spears and arrows that you see are very real. It's not for nothing that everybody in these islands fears the Jarawa. They've been nice to us, but don't take their good nature for granted. Be respectful!'

The chattering group of adults had dispersed. Aditya saw the thin-faced man and the boy who had escorted them walk down the clearing and squat beside a lady who was sitting next to a wooden bucket. Her hand was dipped inside the bucket, and she seemed to be stirring something inside.

Another man, holding a bunch of arrows, sauntered to where a woman sat with a baby suckling at her breast. He settled himself beside a stone whose surface was flat, like a table. Selecting one of his arrows, he laid it on the stone, and grasping a stone lying nearby, began beating the arrowhead, shaping and working it.

'I think the mussels are ready,' said Chitra, looking at the simmering vessel.

The children were crowded around the pan. A comely young lady with typical short, curly hair walked up and sat beside them. She had beautiful, perfectly formed features, and all she wore was a necklace made of cowrie shells. Reaching out, she put her hand into the pan and plucking out a mussel, offered it to Aditya. Smiling his thanks, Aditya reached out and picked it from her fingers only to yell and drop it instantly.

The children burst into spontaneous laughter and so did the lady.

Chitra laughed too.

One of the children dipped his hand into the boiling pan and fished out another mussel. Aditya gingerly accepted it, and much to the amusement of the gathered children, he tossed it from hand to hand, allowing it to cool. When it had cooled sufficiently, he pulled the two ends apart and imitating what a few of the children were doing, scooped out the meat inside and placed it in his mouth. Aditya nodded appreciatively, enjoying the salty taste.

The children kept up a constant supply of mussels. Chitra, too, couldn't handle the steaming shells. Spreading her soiled handkerchief on the ground, she dropped them to cool before splitting and devouring them.

'Nice as these people are, we can't stay here too long,' said Aditya, after appreciatively consuming several mussels. 'We'll have to move on soon.'

Chitra nodded her agreement. 'It's still afternoon, so if we leave now, we could make it to the Trunk Road by

dark. I'm ready any time you are, but how are we going to go about it?'

'They're not treating us like captives. I think we should be able to leave if we want to. I'll speak with the man who brought us here.'

'You're going to speak to him?'

'You know . . . sign language . . . body language. Whatever.'

Chitra smiled. 'Try your luck. I'll wait here.'

Aditya rose and crossed to where the thin-faced man and the boy were squatting with the lady and her wooden bucket. The bucket apparently contained some kind of paint, and it was being applied to the boy's chest. The paint was a white, clay-like substance, and the lady was spreading it evenly across the boy's chest. Aditya pulled off his shirt as he sat next to them. He grinned and pointed at his chest.

The lady laughed and so did the man. She dipped her fingers in the wooden bucket and reaching forward spread the chalky substance on Aditya's brow.

The boy's face crumpled with mirth, and he guffawed so loudly that the other Jarawa came running to see what the fun was about.

The children around the fire ran to join the crowd, and collecting a handful of mussels, Chitra followed. As she walked towards the gathering, she saw two shadow-like figures enter the clearing. Both were young men. One was stark naked like all the other Jarawa, but the other wore a pair of pink shorts and a large matching hat with floral designs. A watch strap, minus the watch, was strapped to his wrist and a pair of torn sneakers dangled from his hand. Both newcomers stopped dead in their tracks when they saw Chitra. Ignoring them she walked towards the gathering.

Aditya's face had already been daubed white, and the lady was now smearing the chalk-like paint on his chest. The gathered Jarawa were enjoying the spectacle. From the corner of her eye Chitra noticed the oddly dressed Jarawa youth halt near her. Though Chitra could sense he was staring intently at her she averted her eyes, refusing to return his gaze.

The crowd cackled as Aditya, paint job completed, rose to his feet. The thin-faced Jarawa placed a long, wooden object on Aditya's chest and pressed it against him. The object had a pattern of precise geometrical rectangles cut into it, like a stencil. A few seconds later the Jarawa pulled it away. The stencil had plucked away the clay, leaving an imprint whose design was identical to that on the stencil. Finding another spot on Aditya's chest, the man placed the stencil and pressed once more.

Absorbed with the proceedings, Chitra had forgotten about the oddly dressed Jarawa youth, but when she turned, her eyes came to rest on him. A sixth sense warned Chitra about the man. His presence was unsettling. She made to turn away, but his absurd clothes, especially in the midst of the beautiful bare-skinned Jarawa, held her gaze.

Staring insolently at Chitra, the young man spoke: 'Deepika,' he said.

Chitra looked uncomprehendingly at him.

He was a foot shorter than Chitra, and as she looked down at him, an arrogant smirk appeared on his face. 'Alia,' he said and followed on with, 'Anushka.'

Was he trying to address her? The names he spoke were common Indian names.

'Chitra,' she said, forcing herself to smile. There was something about his face that made Chitra uneasy. Unlike the simple, innocent expressions around her, there was a craftiness and cunning about him.

The youth wasn't interested in her name. 'Aishwarya, Katrina', he continued.

The sequence of names finally clicked. The oddly dressed man was mouthing names of popular Indian film actresses.

'No,' said Chitra, waving her hand. 'Me Chitra.'

But disregarding her reply, the young man addressed her rapidly in his language.

Chitra smiled and shook her head.

The young man was speaking loudly, and others were turning to see what the matter was. Chitra continued to smile and shake her head. The youth, still jabbering loudly, walked over to the wooden bucket. Dipping his hand inside he crossed to Chitra and applied paint on her face. Though Chitra didn't like his touch, she allowed him to smear her cheeks. But when he began pulling up her T-shirt to apply it on her body, she firmly pushed him away.

The youth staggered back, and his flowery hat fell to the ground.

Children giggled. Others whispered and a few women talked loudly.

The youth began to jabber again. There was anger in his voice and a dangerous glitter in his eyes. He was gesturing with his hands, pulling an imaginary T-shirt above his head.

Chitra clearly understood what the youth was demanding, but she wasn't going to comply. She bunched her fists instead.

Aditya spoke soothingly. 'Don't whack him. Calm down. Take it easy.'

The youth snatched his hat from the ground and hearing Aditya's voice turned to him.

'Namaste,' grinned Aditya.

Though the hatted Jarawa's dress sense was comical, his blazing eyes weren't. A couple of women and the thin-faced Jarawa were speaking to him with disapproving voices. But he paid no attention to them. 'Amitabh Bachan,' he said, staring at Aditya.

'*Nahi*,' said Aditya in Hindi. '*Mera naam*, Aditya.'

'Amitabh Bachan,' repeated the Jarawa, and he strode towards Aditya, halting only when his nose was an inch from his chest.

The brim of the Jarawa's hat pressed against Aditya's throat. Aditya stepped back, and as he did, he felt something being removed from his trouser pocket.

His gun!

Aditya reached down, but it was too late—the hatted Jarawa was holding it in his hand.

Chitra stiffened.

There was a loud buzz amongst the watching Jarawa, and they stepped back as the young man brandished the gun. With his finger on the trigger, he pointed the barrel at Aditya's chest.

Chitra clutched her mouth.

There was a vicious snarl on the hatted Jarawa's face as he looked at Aditya.

Aditya grinned weakly back at him.

'Drop it!' shouted Chitra. '*Bandook chod do!*'

The Jarawa turned his head to Chitra. A sinister grin appeared on his face. He adjusted the gun, squaring it against Aditya's chest, and pressed the trigger.

Chitra screamed.

The assembled Jarawa reacted too. Except for the children, the others flung themselves to the ground, pressing their ears with their hands. Chitra screamed again when the trigger was pressed once more. But despite the hatted youth's repeated efforts, nothing happened.

Aditya, whose throat had iced over, breathed again. His lungs pumped hard, and he gasped as he stared at the now grinning young man. The hatted Jarawa tossed the gun away. This caused another scramble amongst the Jarawa on the ground. With a sudden lunge, the youth reached for Aditya's other pocket and extracted the penknife it contained.

But Aditya had had enough. He wasn't going to remain a bystander this time round. He grasped the Jarawa, and holding him in a grip of steel, he pried the knife away. Aditya shoved hard, sending the young man stumbling. Turning to the thin-faced Jarawa on the ground beside him, he lavished on him a smile of genuine warmth and placed the penknife in his hands.

'Take it,' said Aditya, folding his hands. 'My gift to you.'

A happy grin broke on the Jarawa's face, and he said something that Aditya presumed to be a 'thank you'. But an angry expression clouded his features as he rose and looked over Aditya's shoulder.

A crowd had gathered around the pink-hatted Jarawa. The men and women of the community had surrounded him. The lady with the cowry necklace was there too, and her voice rose above the rest as she angrily admonished him.

Chitra appeared beside Aditya and grabbed his arm.

'The crazy idiot!' she gasped. 'He almost killed you!'

'I thought I was a goner,' admitted Aditya.

Chitra clung tightly to his arm. She blinked, holding back tears. 'What happened, why didn't the gun go off?' There was a tremor in her voice.

'We swam to the shore, remember? It got soaked. The mechanism probably hasn't dried out. Either that or the bullets have run out.'

'I want to get out of here,' said Chitra determinedly. 'The lunatic scares me. I don't want to hang about with him here. He might stick an arrow into one of us next.'

'True,' agreed Aditya. 'He's capable of that and a lot worse. It's getting late too; we have to move on. I'll try and communicate our intentions . . . though I'm not sure how.'

'Try the man who brought us here,' suggested Chitra. 'The one you gave your knife to.'

The thin-faced Jarawa, his newly acquired knife in hand, was standing at the edge of the group that surrounded the hatted young man. He beamed when Aditya stopped by his side.

'We go,' said Aditya to him, in Hindi. Walking to Chitra's side he held her hand and together they strode to the edge of the clearing. Turning, he caught the Jarawa's eye and pointed to the forest. 'We go,' he repeated.

The tall Jarawa comprehended. The lady with the cowrie necklace had been watching Aditya, and she understood too. She ran across to them and holding each by the hand, pulled them back into the clearing.

'Oh no,' groaned Chitra.

'Smile,' urged Aditya. 'Don't worry, I'll be firm.'

The children milled about them, some of them tugging at Chitra.

They were separated, the children holding on to Chitra and the cowrie-necklaced lady clinging to Aditya.

'The lady seems to like you,' called Chitra, as the children pulled her away.

'My irresistible charm,' smirked Aditya.

'Sure,' returned Chitra. 'Your sweaty, dirty, unshaven charm.'

When the lady finally released Aditya, he found himself beside the thin-faced Jarawa once more. Aditya turned to the man and spoke.

'Burma,' he said loudly. 'Burma badmaash.' Aditya cupped his hand like a gun and pointed at himself. 'Bang, bang,' he said. 'Burma bang, bang.' He ran a finger across his throat. 'Burma kill, Burma come.' He pointed at the forest.

The thin-faced man said something. The other Jarawa gathered nearby spoke too, and they soon gathered in a conference. The hatted Jarawa was ignored. He stood apart, glaring at Chitra and Aditya. The discussion turned out to be a long one with all the Jarawa participating.

'What's with the lunatic?' asked Aditya, looking at him. 'Why is he behaving so strangely?'

'I've been trying to figure him out,' replied Chitra. 'I think he's one of those who hang about the Uttara Jetty. You always find a few Jarawa loafing around there. They do nothing except stare at the bus passengers as they come and go. Some of them learn a little Hindi from the Bush Police. The Bush Police also teach them film songs and from the names he called us I guess they pick up names of film stars too.'

'He knows his film stars all right,' agreed Aditya.

'It all points to the jetty,' said Chitra. 'He is one of the good-for-nothings who hang about there. Look at him—absurd isn't he, in his pink shorts and stupid hat? I wonder where he got the hat from. It doesn't look Indian—must have taken it off a foreigner.' Chitra paused. 'However flowery the hat is, it can't conceal his meanness. He is a nasty piece of work.'

'A bloody murderer.' Aditya spoke feelingly. 'He would have killed me if that gun had gone off.'

Chitra shuddered. 'He gives me the creeps. He's not like the others who are friendly and decent.'

'Friendly and talkative,' said Aditya, marvelling at the still continuing discussion. 'They like to chat, don't they?'

Chitra laughed. 'Yes. Look at them. They're all talking together. There doesn't seem to be any leader amongst them.'

'Like our Indian Parliament,' quipped Aditya.

The discussion ended presently. Turning away from the group, the thin-faced Jarawa summoned two young boys and spoke rapidly to them. The lady with the cowrie necklace hurried to the huts and returned with a wooden bucket in her hands. Making her way to Chitra and Aditya, she halted before them and pulled back the lid. There was a dark, syrupy liquid inside.

'Honey!' exclaimed Chitra, smiling at the lady. Dipping her finger inside the bucket, Chitra licked it.

The lady grasped Chitra's hand and submerged it in the honey. Chitra's hand dripped as she withdrew it. Lifting her arm she sucked at the delicious, sweet liquid.

Aditya scooped out a handful when the lady offered him the bucket. Brushing aside a dead bee he brought his hands to his lips. 'Umm . . . the nicest way to eat honey,' he said, slurping delightedly.

'You bet,' said Chitra.

After several helpings from the bucket, they drank deeply from a plastic water bottle that the children thoughtfully provided.

The thin-faced Jarawa was waiting for them. Beside him stood the two young Jarawa who had been summoned earlier. Aditya recognised one of them as the thick-nosed boy from the beach. The older Jarawa pointed to the boys and spoke rapidly, gesturing often. Chitra caught the word 'jetty', which was repeated several times during his speech.

Chitra spoke after the man had had his say. 'Jetty,' she said, and the man nodded. She pointed at the two young boys, then at herself and Aditya, and repeated the word, 'Jetty.'

The man smiled and nodded vigorously.

'We are being provided an escort to Uttara Jetty,' Chitra informed Aditya.

'The place where the ferry is?'

Chitra nodded. 'These two are going to show us the way.'

Aditya turned to the thin-faced man. 'Dhanyawad,' he said, smiling.

The man beamed from ear to ear.

All the Jarawa collected to bid them goodbye. The children were laughing; some were singing.

Looking about the smiling faces, Aditya noticed that the troublemaking, hatted Jarawa was absent.

Chitra embraced the lady with the cowrie necklace, who laughed and hugged her. Aditya folded his hands and bowed. Her face dimpled as she replicated Aditya's gesture. The thin-faced Jarawa hurried to the huts and returned with two slender wooden sticks with pointed steel ends and presented one each to Chitra and Aditya.

'Dhanyawad,' thanked Aditya, eagerly accepting his.

Chitra bowed when she was presented hers.

The two young boys were waiting.

Waving goodbye, they walked towards the forest. Chitra's throat started to lump as she followed the boys. She paused at the edge of the clearing, her eyes taking in the primitive huts, the burning logs, the aluminium pans, the plastic bottles and the wild boar trophies.

The naked, smiling people waving goodbye were the dreaded Jarawa—the most feared and mistrusted tribe of the Andaman Islands. They were branded as fierce and cold-blooded, a bloodthirsty people who killed for the flimsiest of reasons. But she and Aditya had discovered the other side of the Jarawa. The tribals had saved their lives and fed and looked after them. Now they were warmheartedly speeding them on their way. Amongst these people she had discovered a quality of friendship that was innocent and simple. During the short period of time she had spent in their home, bonds had been forged that she would never forget. Her eyes blurred as she waved her final goodbye. As she turned away, she promised herself she would return one day.

DECEPTION

The singing of the Jarawa faded. Giant trees cut off the sun once more. In spite of the freshness of the shaded forest, Chitra and Aditya were soon sweating freely. The Jarawa boys were moving briskly, and they had to work hard to stay level with them. The bare bodies of the Jarawa glistened with wetness too, but their cracking pace did not waver.

Chitra and Aditya were decidedly grateful when after a lengthy march their jungle-bred counterparts suddenly pulled up. While they huffed and clutched their sides, the jungle boys stood still, looking back along the way they had come. Cocking arrows to their bowstrings they stood silent and alert. At first, Chitra and Aditya stared blankly, but when they strained their ears, they detected a distant shuffling sound. The sound grew steadily louder. The Jarawa boys began to talk, and there were flashes of pink in the forest.

Aditya groaned. 'I hope that's not who I think it is.'

'The lunatic,' whispered Chitra, confirming Aditya's fears.

A colourful hat and pink shorts were visible in the distance.

'What on earth does he want?' muttered Aditya.

'Maybe he wants to come along to Uttara,' hazarded Chitra. 'The jetty must be his hangout joint. My guess is that he wants to tag along.'

The young man still wore his hat and shorts, and like before, he incongruously held his shoes in his hands, running barefoot. A long spear was clasped along with the shoes. The insolent smirk was unchanged on his dark face.

'What is his problem?' railed Chitra, as the two other Jarawa barked questions at him. 'Why does he loathe us so?'

Aditya shrugged. 'Beats me. He took an instant dislike to us.'

'A murderous dislike,' hissed Chitra, watching the three Jarawa. 'It's possible that people tease and trouble him at the jetty. That could explain his odd behaviour. He strikes me as the sort who wants to be accepted by people who wear clothes. It could be that he isn't being accepted, and people instead make fun of him.'

'Do you blame them?' asked Aditya. 'Look at the way he's dressed! I'd laugh if I saw him at the jetty.'

'That's what's poisoning his mind,' said Chitra. 'The rejection and the scorn must be hard to take. In his eyes we belong to the same clothed community that refuses to accept him. It could be he's venting his frustrations on us.'

The Jarawa conference had concluded, and the hatted man was waving them forward with his spear.

Aditya stared stonily at the unwanted intruder. 'We're out of luck with this guy. We can't seem to get rid of him. You go first, Chitra, I'll walk between him and you.'

Chitra fell in line behind the Jarawa boys. Aditya followed behind her, and the hatted Jarawa brought up the rear. The boys in front quickly reverted to their gruelling pace. Chitra and Aditya followed, sweating and panting. But now in addition to their exertions, they had to put up with crude laughter every time one of them stumbled or fell.

Unsettled by the presence of the loony Jarawa, Chitra hoped the walk would end soon, and surprisingly it did. This time the sound that distracted their escorts was obvious. There was a loud scrambling noise followed by several high-pitched bleats.

The Jarawa began to chatter once more. The hatted one spoke the loudest. Hooves pounded, and they saw dark flashes through the underbrush. Soon it was only the hatted Jarawa who was rattling away. The two boys were nodding their heads, apparently agreeing with what the lunatic was saying.

One of the boys suddenly set off, racing like a bloodhound in the direction of the disturbance. The second turned and speaking rapidly addressed Chitra and Aditya. He waved his hands, pointing alternately between them and the hatted youth. Then he turned and dashed off after his partner.

'Gaya,' said the hatted Jarawa, smirking.

'Gone where?' asked Aditya, in Hindi.

'Dukkar,' came the reply.

'They've gone to hunt pigs?' said Aditya, trying to make sense of the events.

'Dukkar,' repeated the hatted one, and raising his spear, thrust it repeatedly at the ground.

'They've gone hunting,' confirmed Chitra. 'The Jarawa love wild boar. Hunting pigs is their favourite pastime. I frankly don't mind, Aditya. We'll wait here, I can do with the rest.'

But the hatted youth waved his spear at Chitra and shook his head at her as she sank to the ground. 'Chalo, chalo!' he shouted in Hindi. He gesticulated energetically, pointing along the path they had been following.

Chitra ignored the man and finding a tree trunk she leaned against it.

But the man continued to jabber, repeating the word 'chalo' and pointing at the forest with his spear.

'He seems keen to keep going,' said Aditya.

Chitra snorted. 'Good. I hope he does, we can do without him.'

'You know, I think he's trying to tell us that the other two aren't coming back.'

Chitra stared incredulously. 'What? They can't have gone away and left us. Not in the hands of this lunatic! I don't believe him.'

The hatted man continued to prattle, but Chitra sat firmly on the ground ignoring him.

Aditya wasn't as sure as Chitra. The sign language of the second Jarawa boy before he rushed off after his mate seemed to bear with what the hatted man was trying to convey. He knelt beside Chitra and explained his fears.

Chitra refused to believe him. 'I'm waiting,' she said shortly. 'They'll come back soon; you'll see!'

The hatted man ranted and raved. He shook his spear and repeated the word 'chalo' over and over again. Then, like an ear-splitting music system suddenly switched off, he turned silent. After a withering glare, he stomped off into the forest without looking back.

'Good riddance!' called Chitra, behind his disappearing back.

Sighing, Aditya flopped beside Chitra. He looked up, searching for the sun amidst the canopy. 'We have about an hour of sunlight remaining,' he estimated. 'We could get stuck in the dark if we wait too long.'

'The boys will come back,' said Chitra stubbornly.

Aditya spoke evenly. 'We'll give them fifteen minutes. They left five minutes back, twenty minutes should be enough for a pig hunt. If they don't return by then we leave.'

Chitra stifled a yawn. 'Okay. I could do with the rest. I'm dozing off. Wake me when they return.'

Aditya shut his eyes too. Birds chirped and a kingfisher, calling noisily, flew by. Leaves fell from the canopy, spiralling lazily to the ground. Aditya rested, collecting his thoughts.

Their escape was disastrous for Patrick. If Chitra and he made it back to civilisation the navy and coast guard would swoop down on his hideout. Patrick was obviously a worried man, and Aditya wondered what could possibly be going on in his mind. After a lengthy deliberation, he concluded that the man was left with only two realistic courses of action: stake everything on the search for them

or start abandoning his hideout. Aditya was inclined to believe that Patrick would continue with the search. The man didn't strike him as the sort who would give up easily.

But if Patrick was indeed searching for them, where would he concentrate his efforts? The forest was too large a place, and in any case the Jarawa wouldn't allow him in. That left only the coastline and the Trunk Road. Could Patrick and his men already be patrolling the villages and settlements along the Trunk Road? There was every likelihood, concluded Aditya. It was obvious that Chitra and he would have to make it there if they wanted help. They would have to be cautious when they approached the road.

Patrick was not a small-time crook. The operation they had stumbled upon was a large and well-financed one. The equipment and machinery Aditya had seen at the hideout was impressive and expensive. The storage shed possibly held the key to the set-up. Something unlawful and obviously valuable was being smuggled into the islands and stored in the shed. The mystery would be solved if Chitra and he managed to elude capture. Everything, including Vikram and Alex's fate, depended on their ability to outwit Patrick and his friends. Failure could prove to be disastrously expensive.

Except for the call of birds, the forest was silent. Aditya occasionally heard rustling amidst the leaves on the ground, and when his gaze followed the trail of sound, he sometimes saw lizards. After one particularly noisy run under the leaves he spotted a small green lizard, but when he looked at it, something else caught his eye.

Aditya kneaded Chitra with his elbow. 'Snake!' he hissed.

Chitra's eyes snapped open. She blinked.

'A king,' she whispered in awe. 'Help me God! I can't believe it . . . it's a king—a king cobra!' She grasped Aditya's arm. 'Don't move! He hasn't seen us.'

The snake was long, and its head was crusted with large, conspicuous scales. Aditya recalled Vikram telling him that the king cobra was the largest venomous snake in the world and that it packed a huge amount of venom in its fangs—enough to kill an elephant. A bite was always fatal, resulting in an awful death.

The snake's head was raised. It was eyeing the lizard, and the lizard was staring back at it. It was amazing how still and motionless reptiles could be. If it were not for the quivering of the lizard's throat Aditya could have sworn that the two creatures were carved works of art, placed for effect on the forest floor.

Chitra harboured no doubts that the king cobra was a work of art. 'Wow!' she gasped, still holding Aditya's arm. 'Just look how big it is. It's truly a king . . . so beautiful.'

Aditya made a face. 'Beautiful? How can you call a snake beautiful? Awesome, yes. Maybe magnificent too, but not beautiful!'

The reptile was indeed a magnificent specimen. The scales on its head were yellow. Not a flashy yellow, but a subdued forest shade that contrasted with the scales on its underside, which were pale, like ivory. The king's eyes were black, and they were staring directly at him. To his horror Aditya discovered that Chitra had risen to a crouch, and the snake had noticed her movement.

The snake turned to face them. It raised its head and puffed its body in a gesture that clearly indicated aggression. 'Do we run?' enquired Aditya, in as calm a tone as he could manage.

'No! Don't be stupid! He's not going to do anything to us. What an incredible sight . . . it's puffing and swaying. It's trying to scare us off.'

Chitra, though faced with the most venomous of land snakes, decided to advance on it.

Horrified, Aditya reached out and held her leg. 'Are you crazy?' he whispered.

'I'm not,' protested Chitra. 'Leave me. I just want to get a better look. I'll keep my distance. Promise.'

Aditya reluctantly let go.

At the same moment the king lowered its head and began to slither away. Chitra stepped forward, following the snake. Aditya rose too and walked warily behind Chitra. They tracked the snake, tramping through leaves and vegetation. They halted when it paused and looked back at them. After a long, heart-stopping stare, the king cobra slithered forward once more. It was moving faster now. Aditya heaved a sigh of relief when Chitra halted. Their gaze followed the snake as it undulated through the vegetation. Then, with a loud rustle, it disappeared.

'*Amazing!*' blurted Chitra, her eyes wide with wonder. 'What an incredible sighting!'

'You're mad,' said Aditya, shaking his head. 'Goofy! Nuts! Was I imagining things or were you planning to catch it?'

Chitra laughed. 'Me, catch a king cobra? You've got to be joking. I have a healthy respect for kings. All I wanted was a closer look. You don't know it, but king cobras are extremely shy. You saw that for yourself. All the poor creature wanted was to get away from us. Yet, shy or not, I wouldn't dream of handling a king.'

'Then how come you were prepared to pick up the sea snake last night? Isn't it as deadly as a king cobra?'

'Sea snakes are different. They are creatures of the sea and are out of their element on land. On shore they are dull and move sluggishly. I would never attempt catching one in the sea, but on land they are easy to handle. The king cobra is another matter altogether. They move like lightning when threatened. There are experts who can handle kings. I'm not one of them.'

'My, my,' mocked Aditya. 'Finally, some modesty. Wonder Woman isn't perfect after all.'

Chitra flared with anger. 'Look who's talking!' she hooted. She faced Aditya, hands on her hips. 'What do you know about snakes?' she demanded. 'You can't even handle a harmless rat snake.'

Aditya's face turned red. He didn't like being talked down to.

Chitra held up her hand. 'Don't you start,' she warned. 'You asked for that. You provoked me.'

Aditya breathed hard.

'Forget it,' said Chitra. 'This is not the time or place for a quarrel.' She changed the subject. 'You were right about the Jarawa boys. They aren't coming back. Let's leave. We have to make the most of the light while it lasts. The Trunk Road lies to the east.' Checking the position of the sun, she turned a half-circle. 'That way,' she pointed. 'Away from the setting sun.'

Retrieving their spears, they set off, the sun on their backs. Aditya led the way, setting a pace almost as fast as that of the Jarawa.

'Maybe the loony Jarawa was telling us the truth,' panted Aditya, after several minutes of hard walking.

'That the others wouldn't be returning?'

'Yes. There's no doubt that the boys wanted to hunt the pig. They wouldn't have walked out on us if it weren't for the lunatic. They must have known he was going to the jetty, so they left us with him.'

'Could be,' panted Chitra. 'But I'm much happier without the lunatic. We can find the road on our own.'

Aditya pulled up just as Chitra finished talking and Chitra bumped into him.

She opened her mouth to protest, but the tramp of running feet silenced her. 'Oh no!' she breathed, catching a flash of pink.

It was the hatted Jarawa all right. They saw him through a break in the undergrowth, running as before, with his spear and shoes in his hands. He waved his arms and jabbered loudly as he approached. He halted before them, his dark body shimmering with sweat.

'Jetty,' he said, and pointed a direction different to the one they had been pursuing. The route he indicated was perpendicular to theirs.

'He's pointing south,' said Chitra, in a puzzled tone.

Aditya raised his hand and pointed south too.

The hatted Jarawa danced excitedly, jigging his head and repeating the word 'jetty' over and over again. Starting southwards, he strode a short distance. Then turning, he looked at them.

'He wants us to follow him,' said Aditya, interpreting the Jarawa's actions.

'I'm not sure I want to,' said Chitra.

'I think we should. He seems to be sure of himself.'

Chitra pouted. 'I don't like him.'

'Nor do I. But it's going to get dark soon. We're lost in any case. Let's give him a chance.'

Chitra wasn't convinced, but Aditya had set off after the hatted man, and she reluctantly followed.

The Jarawa set a cracking pace, faster than that of their earlier escorts, and Chitra and Aditya had to strain harder than before to keep up. So nimble was the youth on his bare feet that the shoes in his hands looked entirely superfluous, like add-on flippers for a fish.

The run reminded Chitra of her morning sprint through the forest. The terrain was an identical expanse of trees, roots, rocks and undergrowth. She had handled the going well then, but now she was beginning to tire. Except for her short nap, she had been on the go since morning. Her thighs hurt and her legs trembled. But the sun was dipping fast, and they had to make the most of the light before it faded.

The glory of the sunset was lost on them under the canopy, all they noticed was a steady fall in visibility. Owls were calling and bats were taking wing when the Jarawa halted. They were silent for a while as they all struggled to catch their breath.

'Jetty?' questioned Aditya, holding his hips and breathing deeply.

The hatted Jarawa did not reply. He smiled instead.

'Jetty?' asked Aditya, once more.

The Jarawa laughed and shook his head.

'Stupid idiot!' expostulated Aditya.

Chitra spoke worriedly. 'Has he been taking us for a ride?'

'Burma badmaash,' sniggered the hatted youth.

'What?' asked Aditya, not comprehending.

'Burma badmaash,' he repeated and cackled with laughter.

'He's gone crazy,' whispered Chitra.

Aditya advanced menacingly on the hatted man. But the Jarawa backed away, chortling and sneering all the while.

'Burma badmaash,' he repeated once more, and turning, he ran.

Aditya and Chitra stared speechlessly after him. The Jarawa was generating an astonishing amount of noise as he ran. Pausing some distance from them, he yelled, chanted, whooped, whistled and danced.

'Demented,' said Aditya, staring bewilderedly.

'What an incredible capacity for noise,' marvelled Chitra.

'A heavy metal band could do with somebody like him.'

The Jarawa effortlessly maintained his cacophony, increasing and lowering his tempo in a clumsy musical manner. He paused suddenly, and as silence swept the forest, a look of intense concentration came to his face.

The engrossed expression lasted barely a minute, and then a hideous cackle sprang forth from him.

'He, he, he . . . Burma . . . Burma . . . badmaash,' he chuckled. Leering tauntingly at them, he turned and ran. Like a hare, he pelted through the forest, cackling all the while.

'Remind me never to trust lunatics,' stated Aditya bitterly, as the laughter faded.

'And remind me not to trust your judgement again,' said Chitra meaningfully.

Aditya was silent.

Chitra sighed. 'It's all right. I didn't mean it that way. Sorry.'

Aditya looked at the ground.

'We'll have to make a decision soon,' continued Chitra. 'Either we walk in the dark or we find a place to spend the night.'

Moonlight was making its presence felt as it filtered through the trees. Crickets were calling, and shadows crept everywhere.

Aditya broke his silence. 'We have to alert the navy as soon as possible,' he said. 'The earlier Vikram and Alex are rescued, the better. Let's make for the road.'

'Right,' said Chitra.

'Moonlight will help us. Let's not waste—' Aditya halted in mid-sentence.

A faint sound had disturbed him. Chitra had heard it too and they both turned, staring in the direction of the noise. But all they saw were shadows and shafts of moonlight.

Chitra drew closer to Aditya. An owl called, a soft musical call.

'There's something out—' But once more Aditya did not complete his sentence.

Shadows were moving in the forest. There were several shadows, and they were all around them.

Chitra's voice quavered. 'They are human,' she whispered, 'not animals.' She grabbed Aditya's arm as he stepped forward to pluck his spear from the ground. 'Wait!' she hissed.

The shadows were indeed two-legged, and they tightened around them from all sides, like a knot. The shadows were short. But they weren't the Jarawa. Their hair was different, not curly or short. Some had long locks that hung to their shoulders. One of the shadows was holding a gun, and the others held knives that flashed in the moonlight.

POACHERS

A knife was pressed hard into Aditya's back, and he was pushed forward.

'*Walk!*' hissed Chitra, when she saw the gleam of defiance in Aditya's eyes. 'There's a knife in my back too.'

Resistance was useless, the shadows were far too many. Two led the way. Others hemmed Chitra and Aditya from all sides, jostling them along.

The shadows laughed, and there was plenty of chatter. Their words were musical in part and softly spoken, very different from the expressive Jarawa vocabulary. Moonlight revealed their features as East Asian, and their skin was far paler than that of the Jarawa.

After a brief march, the crackling of leaves underfoot lessened. Aditya noticed that they were walking along a path and that the ground was damp. The smell of rotting fish pervaded their nostrils. A roofed structure appeared, and they were steered into it.

They were instructed to sit back-to-back. A rope was produced. Their hands were tied behind their backs;

individually first, and then to one another. So tightly were they bound that if Aditya moved his hands, Chitra was forced to shift hers too.

'Are they Burmese?' enquired Aditya, as their bonds were checked.

'Yes,' replied Chitra, from behind him. 'We've stumbled on to a pack of Burmese poachers.'

The men moved away, leaving behind one of their number to look after them.

'Poachers?' asked Aditya.

'They have to be,' said Chitra. 'The rotten smell is that of sea cucumbers. The ground, if you noticed, turned wet on the last part of the walk. We are at the edge of a creek. I can tell by the shadows of the trees ahead that they are mangrove.'

'Is this why the loony Jarawa kept saying Burma badmaash?'

Chitra spoke bitterly. 'Yes, he deliberately led us here. The slimy so and so! Everyone at the settlement knew we were on the run from the Burmese. So, purely out of spite, he led us to where he knew there was a Burmese camp, and by dancing and screaming at the top of his voice, he alerted them.'

Aditya smiled in the darkness. 'His plan worked well. Pity he wasn't around to savour its success.'

Chitra snorted. 'I'm sure he saw it all happen. He must have been skulking amongst the trees, watching gleefully.'

'Who are these people anyway?' asked Aditya.

'Burmese peasants. They travel all the way here from their homes in Myanmar. They come to collect trepang. Trepang is the harmless sea cucumber.'

'Sea cucumbers . . . I remember them from the lagoons of Lakshadweep,'* recalled Aditya. 'They were always curled in the sand, like pipe sections or hoses that somebody had discarded. Why would anyone want to collect them? Are they tasty?'

'Umm . . . the Burmese believe so, they are a delicacy there. The Burmese love them so much that they have exhausted their natural supply—the poor creature is probably extinct on their coasts. So, they come here to collect them. They make a lot of money with each trip and though it is dangerous—many of them have been caught and jailed—they keep coming. Jarawa creeks suit them because they are rarely patrolled.'

'The Jarawa don't mind?'

'Of course, they mind. They don't like it at all. They clash often with them. Why do you think my "Burma badmaash" worked? They hate the Burmese.'

'You are a fountain of information.' Aditya spoke with grudging respect. 'Is there anything you don't know about the islands?'

'Lots,' laughed Chitra. 'But yes, I've learned a bit. Six months is a long time in the Andamans.'

They turned silent, resting companionably against one another.

It was several minutes before Chitra spoke. 'Stop it!' she exclaimed irritably. 'Your back is so nice and comfy. Don't spoil it by twitching and fidgeting like a monkey.'

---

* Refer to *Lakshadweep Adventure*.

Aditya thumped his feet on the ground. 'Aren't you getting bitten? The bloody mosquitoes!'

'*Sandflies!*' exclaimed Chitra, rocking violently. 'Oh no! Sandflies again! We've had it, Aditya!'

There was no escape for them. They were sitting ducks for the skin-perforating insects.

Aditya squeezed his eyes shut. 'They are worse than bees,' he grimaced. 'This is torture. I'd give anything to have my hands free.'

'Free hands don't help; you need free legs. The only way to lose them is to escape to sea or to run inland, where they don't come. Those thoughtless fools, our captors, they've cut both options. But we're not done for. They'll cool off after a while. Stop twitching! Grin and bear them.'

'Grin—' muttered Aditya. 'The air is so thick with them that they are clogging my nostrils as I breathe . . . and you want me to grin.'

'Don't grin then. Just stop jerking about like a puppet. Curl into a pillow instead. A nice cuddly one. I want to take a nap.'

Aditya clenched his jaw and lowered his head. To his surprise, his eyelids began to droop. The extent of his weariness became apparent to him. Fortunately, the stinging pinpricks of the sandflies faded to the back of his consciousness, and like Chitra, he lapsed into a deep sleep.

He had no idea how long he slept, but when he woke, the sandflies had gone. The stillness of Chitra's body and her even breathing indicated she was still asleep. Aditya looked about him, wondering what had disturbed him.

Voices. He heard voices and the tramp of feet.

Aditya couldn't see the approaching men. He was tied sideways, facing away from them. Footsteps entered the hut, and Aditya shut his eyes as torchlight was directed on his face. The beam blinded him. When it was finally switched off, he blinked several times before he could see again.

Two men were squatting before him. They were shadows. Darkness masked their features. One of the shadows spoke, and Aditya discovered he could understand the softly spoken words. The language was Hindi, a halting, accented Hindi.

'Who are you?' asked the shorter shadow.

'We are school kids.' Aditya spoke in Hindi too.

'What are you doing here?'

'A Jarawa brought us here,' replied Aditya. 'He promised to take us to Uttara Jetty but instead he abandoned us here.'

'You are hungry,' said the man. His Hindi wasn't very good. 'I give food. You eat.'

Chitra had woken, and Aditya felt her body stiffen at the mention of food. Aditya smiled and replied, 'Yes, hungry. Thank you very much.'

Aditya discovered the presence of a third man when a hand reached out between Chitra and him and loosened their bonds.

The man who spoke Hindi directed them to sit cross-legged at the centre of the hut. A pot was placed before them along with a plastic bottle filled with water. There was rice in the pot mixed with a spicy fish curry. Though cold and watery, the curry and rice were nourishing, and Chitra and Aditya licked their fingers, relishing their unexpected meal.

The Hindi-speaking man had risen to his feet. A lungi-like cloth was draped across his hips, and above, he wore a ragged T-shirt. He was unarmed, but the two other men casually displayed weapons. One held a gun, and the other had a knife tucked prominently in his belt.

While they ate a torch-beam appeared in the darkness. It was distant, and they saw mangrove trees illuminated in its glow. The beam advanced steadily, and as it drew nearer, the Hindi-speaking man stepped out. Still enjoying their food, Chitra and Aditya watched. The approaching torch-beam and the Hindi-speaking man halted when they drew level. A conversation ensued. After a while, the voices turned angry and loud, and it sounded more like an argument than a discussion. The newcomer was taller than the man with the lungi. The beam from his torch revealed long hair that fell to his shoulders and a headband.

Aditya spoke between mouthfuls. 'They're probably discussing what to do with us.'

Chitra chewed a fishbone. 'The tall guy with the headband doesn't look too happy.

Aditya grinned. 'Ah . . . forget about them. Enjoy the food instead.'

The argument ended shortly after they completed their meal. The man with the headband stomped away, and the Hindi-speaking man returned to the hut. Stooping, he squatted before them. He gazed quietly at them, not saying a word.

'Err . . . nice meal,' said Aditya, in Hindi. 'Dhanyawaad.'

The man smiled. His face was heavily crinkled with lines running across it.

'He seems to be a nice old man,' murmured Chitra, in English.

The man cleared his throat. 'We are leaving tonight,' he said.

Chitra and Aditya nodded, though not understanding what he was talking about.

'We have been here many days. For two moons, collecting shells and sea cucumber.'

'You have collected lots of trepang?' asked Chitra, in Hindi.

'Yes, we have enough, and now it is time to return. We leave for Myanmar tonight.'

Chitra nodded.

'I want to leave you here so that you can go to Uttara Jetty tomorrow. But Than—man I talking to—he say no. He say you tell coastguard, navy and they come for us.'

Aditya spoke earnestly. 'We won't tell anybody. You've been nice to us. We promise not to say anything.'

'I tell Than that but he no agree. He say to take you out to sea and leave you there. We gone then, before you can reach navy from there.'

'But—' cried Chitra. 'Don't do that. There is no need, we won't tell anybody.'

The man lowered his eyes. 'No can do,' he said softly. 'Than is chief. But I look after you, no worry.'

'You don't understand—' began Chitra, but the man cut her off.

'Than is chief,' he repeated, shaking his head.

Aditya flicked his eyes about him, searching the dark forest.

The Burmese spotted Aditya's probing look. 'No escape,' he warned. 'Fifty men here. They catch you, beat you.'

'Forget about it, Aditya,' said Chitra. 'You don't stand a chance. These guys flit like birds through the forest. That's what my dad's friend says. He should know. He's a coastguard officer and has busted many Burmese camps.'

Aditya shook his head. 'Burmese, Burmese everywhere,' he muttered darkly. 'We can't get away from them. I have seen so many Burmese faces in the last few days that I'm beginning to wonder if this is a Jarawa reserve or a Burmese playground.'

Chitra laughed. 'It's true, there are lots of Burmese here. Dad says there are many hundreds of them in the islands at any given time, poaching for sea cucumber and shell. Many get caught. I've seen captured ones at Port Blair. They are all held at Aberdeen Bazaar chowky.'

'Aberdeen Bazaar,' said the Hindi-speaking man, his eyes lighting up.

Chitra looked at him. 'You know Aberdeen Bazaar?'

'Port Blair,' said the man enthusiastically. 'I there for two years at Aberdeen Bazaar Police Station. Coastguard catch me, put me in police station. I learn Hindi there. Long time before plane take me back to Myanmar.'

'And you're back again?' said Aditya. 'Suppose coastguard catches you once more?'

The man's face crinkled again. 'I very poor. Everybody here very poor, no money . . . big businessman in Myanmar offer us money to bring sea cucumber from Andaman. Good money . . . so we come.'

'But you get caught and sent to jail,' said Chitra.

'I caught twice,' said the man proudly. 'Many people here caught before. We still come. My son in Aberdeen jail just now—' The man paused. 'You go Port Blair?' he asked.

'If you let us,' said Aditya, his voice loaded with sarcasm.

'You take letter for my son, I write.'

'Sure,' said Chitra.

The man spoke rapidly in Burmese to the others outside the hut. One of them replied loudly, joy igniting his face.

The Hindi-speaking man turned to them. 'That man has father in jail,' he explained. 'My name John, my son is Joseph. You give my letter and all other letters to Joseph. Okay?'

'Sure,' replied Chitra. 'No problem.'

'I get pen and paper.' John rose. 'You wait. Two men guarding. Please . . . no try escape, no trouble.'

Chitra looked at Aditya.

'All right,' sighed Aditya. 'No escape. Promise.'

It turned out that there were four people in the group whose relatives were being held at the Aberdeen jail, and the letters, neatly wrapped and sealed in a plastic bag, were presented to them a half-hour later.

'Waterproof,' said John, handing them the packet. 'No lose, okay?'

Chitra zipped the package in her pouch. She pointed at her pouch. 'This waterproof too, no problem.'

'Thank you,' said John, bowing. 'Camp close down,' he continued. 'We leave soon, you come.'

'We don't want to come,' protested Aditya. 'Leave us here.'

John shook his head solemnly. 'No can do. But I speak to Than. Many people speak to Than. People happy about letters, tell him to trust you. He agree no take you out to sea, only to end of creek. We leave you there with boat. Okay?'

Aditya and Chitra looked at one another.

'That's better than before,' reasoned Chitra.

Aditya shrugged. 'Let's follow him.'

John led the way along a wet path that turned progressively slushier. When it deteriorated to a mud pool, they found themselves walking on logs raised above the slush. They passed shadowy structures that looked like huts. The logs led them through the camp, to mangrove trees, and then out to where moonlight gleamed on water. Two boats were floating side by side. They were longer and wider than dungis and were roofed with bamboo slats. There were several people in the boats, and a voice shouted out at them.

John yelled a reply. 'Everybody ready now,' he said, turning. 'We leave, come.'

'Back to the mud,' sighed Chitra, as the logs ended, and she stepped into the swamp.

'Ee-yuck,' grunted Aditya, following her into the dark, slimy water.

They sloshed behind John, wading out to thigh-deep water. Several hands reached out to help them when they reached the boat. The mood inside was jovial. Men patted them on their backs and smiled broadly. Some laughed boisterously, others sang. The boat shuddered as its motor sprang to life. There were triumphant cries, and the occupants of both boats started clapping.

'Everybody happy!' shouted John, as he led them to a corner. 'We going home!'

The moon had washed the sky ivory-white. Like a celestial searchlight, it shed pearly radiance on the creek and surrounding forest. The boats moved forward, and Aditya caught flashes of its glittering disc through the branches of the trees lining the creek.

The creek was narrow to begin with, but after several loops it broadened, and the speed of the boats picked up.

'How long before you reach Myanmar?' Aditya asked John, shouting to make himself heard.

'Two days. But first we must leave Indian waters. If we caught, we go Aberdeen jail.'

'I told you we won't tell.' Aditya made the sign of a cross. 'Promise.'

'I know,' smiled John. He pointed to the rear of the boat. 'There is boat for you behind. Is leaking, but no problem, it okay. We leave you at creek end, where sea begin. You paddle, someone find you, you okay.'

'What about the Jarawa?' asked Aditya.

'You have boat. They don't come on water. You okay, don't worry.'

'This isn't working out too well,' sighed Chitra, resting her head on Aditya's shoulder.

'Maybe attempting to escape might have been wise.'

'No.' Chitra yawned. 'Not with fifty fleet-footed men. There would have been unpleasantness too, which would have been a shame. They're nice guys actually. They've fed us, they've looked after us and they're giving us a boat. I don't blame them for dropping us at sea. They are safeguarding themselves; the danger is far too great for them. They can't risk even the possibility of an alert before they leave Indian waters.'

'What about trust?' grumbled Aditya. 'Do we look the sort who would betray them?'

'Put yourself in their place, Aditya. With the freedom of so many people in balance, would you trust two unknown teenagers who barged into your camp on the evening you were leaving?'

Aditya grunted but turned silent.

The creek was a ribbon of light. The boats were moving fast now, and the sound of their engines echoed harshly through the forest. The festive atmosphere in the boat had noticeably lessened. There was no more clapping or singing, and the men were talking in subdued tones. Several cigarettes had been lit and were being passed around. Tension was palpable in the air. They were entering the danger zone now. There was always the possibility of an encounter with the navy or the coastguard along the island shores.

The creek grew wider, and Chitra tapped Aditya's shoulder, pointing. In the distance the silver ribbon they were chugging along merged with a glittering mass of water. The glasslike smoothness of the creek began to change. Wrinkles appeared, and Aditya smelt the sea.

Some distance ahead the engines were switched off. No one spoke, and in the silence, they heard the slap of water against the boat hulls. John rose and beckoned Aditya and Chitra to follow. The men made room for them as they stumbled along slippery planks.

A small boat had been lowered in the water. It was so tiny that Chitra wondered how she and Aditya would fit in it. 'You first,' Aditya instructed Chitra.

John handed Chitra a plastic bottle. 'Water,' he said, and to Aditya he handed a large plastic packet. 'Rice inside. You take.'

'Thanks,' beamed Aditya, accepting the welcome gift.

Chitra stepped gingerly into the small boat, crouching and holding its rocking sideboards. Aditya waited for her to settle, and after shaking hands with John, he followed. Holding on to Chitra, he carefully manoeuvred himself and settled beside her. A tin can was handed down to them.

'For water,' shouted John. 'For the boat.' He moved his hands, imitating the action of bailing.

Smiling, Aditya thanked him once more.

'Give letters to my son, Joseph. No forget.'

'We won't,' assured Chitra. 'Goodbye.'

There were two paddles in the boat, and Chitra and Aditya collected one each. The engines started. They waved at the men in the boat, and they waved back.

John's boat moved forward, and Aditya and Chitra felt their tiny boat jerk. They saw a rope attached to its nose.

The rope was taut and John held its other end.

'They're giving us a tow,' cried Chitra. 'There's still some distance to the mouth of the creek.'

'That's if this tub stays afloat till then,' grunted Aditya. 'Look!'

Water was gushing in as if a tap had been opened, and a rapidly enlarging pool was soaking their feet. Grasping the tin, Aditya bent his shoulders and set to work.

The sea was a bowl of silver, flashing and twinkling in the moonlight. The creek widened near its mouth, and the mangrove banks began to slip behind. John shouted from the boat. He tossed the rope he was holding and waved. Chitra waved back as the distance between the boats steadily widened.

THE COAST ONCE MORE

'Yippee!' celebrated Chitra. 'We're on our own again.'
'Yeah,' growled Aditya, pausing from his bailing. 'Just you, me and this leaking tub . . . and a pair of paddles,' he added as an afterthought. 'You better start paddling,' he continued, 'I can't keep this tub afloat forever. Try finding a decent spot to beach on before my arms give way.'

Chitra dipped her paddles and turned the boat parallel to the shore. Fortunately, the sea was calm, and she was able to steer the boat without difficulty. The shore, outlined by trees, wasn't far. She scanned the shadows, searching for a beach or a solid headland where there was no swamp.

Aditya worked frantically with his bailer, but despite his energetic efforts, the pool of water grew deeper. 'We're going to have to abandon ship if we don't land soon,' he warned.

'I see a beach,' panted Chitra. 'Just keep us afloat till we get there.'

Ahead, the trees had stepped back, and a strip of sand sparkled in the moonlight. Chitra paddled and Aditya bailed. Sweat flowed from them, despite a steady breeze. When they drew level with the beach, Chitra turned the boat, pointing its nose shoreward. The swell was mild. Chitra negotiated the surf-line smoothly, and soon the boat was in shallow water. Stepping off, they trudged up the beach, towing their boat behind them.

'Marooned,' gasped Aditya, flopping on the sand.

Chitra pulled the boat as high on the beach as she could and sprawled beside him. She grinned. 'You never see the bright side of things, do you?'

'Yeah,' grunted Aditya. 'And what is it besides the moon that is so bright?'

'The fact that we have food and that we have water.'

Chitra thought for a while. 'And that there are no sandflies or mosquitoes.'

'No sandflies! I didn't notice that. Maybe it will be a pleasant night after all. What about snakes? Are there any sea snakes, like last time?'

Chitra laughed. 'Don't worry. Sea snakes don't come out of the water every day. They are more likely to when the water is cold, like during the monsoon. It's very rare that you see—' Chitra halted in mid-sentence.

'Now what?' Aditya sat up, looking alarmed.

Chitra whispered excitedly. 'There's something in the sand.'

A rounded object, small enough to fit in Chitra's palm, was moving in the shadows. There was a prominent hump-shaped shell on the creature's back. At first Chitra thought it was a hermit crab. But then she saw small flipper-like appendages protruding from its sides.

'A *turtle!*' exclaimed Chitra. 'Aditya, look! A baby turtle!'

Aditya scrambled to his feet and knelt beside Chitra. The tiny creature Chitra had spotted wasn't the only baby turtle on the sand. Aditya saw a second one . . . a third one . . . and looking around him, many more.

'My God!' whispered Chitra. 'A turtle hatching! This is the first time I'm witnessing this.'

The sand was teeming with baby turtles, all scrabbling with their miniscule flippers, working their way towards the sea. And amidst the turtles prowled predatory ghost crabs. Some had grabbed the helpless creatures in their pincers while others, the picky ones, were sizing up those they fancied as a wholesome meal.

Chitra snatched a turtle off the sand as a crab lunged towards it. She picked up a second, a third . . . a handful of baby turtles. Cupping the sand-crusted creatures in her hands, she walked to the sea. Aditya scooped up as many as he could and followed. In knee-deep water they released the reptiles, slipping them gently into the sea.

Moonlight illuminated the hump-shelled hatchlings as they floated in the water. Their flippers—useless in the sand—now paddled them forward. A speeding wave upended the turtles, washing them back to shore. A few, however, managed to stroke their way through the wave. They kept going, swimming resolutely to the ocean. Those that had been swept shoreward by the wave returned in its backwash and paddled furiously seaward.

'Come on!' shouted Chitra. 'Let's help as many as we can.'

And so, Chitra and Aditya pranced on the desolate moonlit beach, snatching tiny turtles from the sand and releasing them in the water. Aditya fondly remembered his best friend as he worked, wishing that Vikram was with them. It was back at Lakshadweep, on a dark moonless night, that a turtle had rescued Vikram from the middle of a vast coral lagoon. Vikram had never forgotten that incident and even today sea turtles were his favourite creatures.*

Earlier, during that same adventure, on a tiny coral island, Vikram, Aditya and an islander named Shaukat had watched a mother turtle emerge from the sea to lay its eggs in the sand. Unlike the tiny creatures he held in his hands, the mother turtle had been big and heavy, reminding Aditya of an armoured battle tank as she heaved herself up the beach. Finding a suitable spot in the sand, she had excavated a nest and laid several eggs. Aditya recalled that they had lost count when the egg numbers crossed one hundred. Then the turtle had covered the nest by flattening sand on it and had trundled back to the lagoon waters.

Here, in the Andaman Sea, another mother turtle had ascended the beach they stood on and had laid her eggs. After their long and lonely incubation, the eggs had hatched, and by sheer chance they had arrived at the beach moments after the hatching.

After several runs to the water with armloads of baby turtles, Chitra and Aditya surveyed the beach, searching for stragglers.

---

* Refer to *Lakshadweep Adventure*.

'That's a lot of offspring for one mamma,' remarked Aditya, reaching down to pick up one more. 'Oh! This one's dead,' he said, and placed it gently back in the sand.

'Lots of offspring is a trademark mother nature solution,' said Chitra. 'Most hatchlings die. So, she increases the number of eggs that a mother bears. Each mother turtle lays over a hundred eggs, and this helps to ensure a decent survival rate. You saw the crabs. If it were daytime, birds would have joined the party too, enjoying a free meal. Once in the water, the creatures of the sea finish off most of the rest. The majority of this lot will die. Only a handful will survive, which is what mother nature wants.'

Aditya gazed out at the moonlit sea. 'I wish Vikram were here. Nature's natural entertainment fascinates him.'

'It fascinates me too,' sighed Chitra. 'It's moments like these that I live for. The king cobra sighting and the turtles have made my day.'

'Don't forget the Jarawa,' Aditya reminded her.

Chitra clapped her forehead. 'How could I!' she cried. 'Yes, the Jarawa too—phew, it's been one heck of a day. I'm dog-tired, but I'm happy.' She turned to Aditya. 'Shall we forget our troubles for the night? Do you mind? Can we just enjoy the beach and the breeze? Let's leave the rest for tomorrow.'

Aditya didn't mind at all. Together they dragged their boat beyond the high-tide line. They then tramped up the beach, settling themselves not far from where the forest began. Bidding good night to one another they fell asleep almost as soon as their heads hit the sand.

It was Aditya who woke first. He blinked as he saw a pale blue sky above him. Turning, he searched for what had disturbed him and spotted a bird. It was a huge white bird with grey wings, and it repeated the call that had roused him as it took off from the sand with something in its mouth.

Aditya gasped. The power and grace of the bird was breathtaking. Long wings heaved mightily as the bird soared skywards with a pair of doomed baby turtles in its beak. An eagle! The bird was a white-bellied sea eagle, the mighty eagle of India's coastline—one of Vikram's favourite birds. The eagle alighted atop a tree at the edge of the beach. Aditya sucked in a deep breath as he stared. There were two other white eagles—much smaller than the majestic specimen that had roused him—sitting quietly on the same tree.

Alerted by the sound of wings again, Aditya turned. Another big bird, a brown one this time, was rising from the sand with a turtle clamped between its curved mandibles. It was also an eagle, possibly a serpent eagle. Aditya wasn't expert enough on birds to be sure.

He then spotted a second brown eagle. It was perched on a tree not far from him, staring at a log of wood on the sand. The rapacious look in its dark eyes hastened Aditya to his feet. Rising, he crossed to the log the bird was gazing at.

A forlorn group of turtles was stranded behind the long bole of wood. Unable to mount the obstacle, they had been left behind in the sand. Gently collecting the exhausted, sand-spattered creatures in his hands, Aditya walked to the sea.

The water was blue, mirroring the sky above. The absence of pink on the horizon indicated that the sun had risen a while ago. Aditya halted in knee-deep water and released the turtles. He watched them paddle furiously before raising his head and scanning the sea.

Aditya blinked once more, not believing his eyes. He could see a boat. It was a low, white boat with a thin, needle-like mast. It wasn't a dungi or a local trawler that he was staring at.

It was a yacht . . . a sleek, expensive, foreign craft.

'CHITRA!' shouted Aditya. 'Look, a boat!'

Chitra was awake. She was sitting up, looking out to sea. 'Aditya—' she cried. 'The eagles!'

Aditya wheeled around. Two snow-white sea eagles were in the water where he had stood, swooping and rising with turtles in their talons. They were the same young pair he had spied in the tree earlier. Aditya glared as they flew away. There was nothing he could do. He had tried his best. Mother nature was selecting her survivors.

Chitra crossed to where Aditya stood, and they both stared out at the boat. With a roar a wave sped up the sand and foamed at their feet.

'Rescue?' asked Chitra.

Aditya grinned. 'Beats running through the jungle.'

Chitra shaded her eyes. 'The boat isn't far. It's not moving. Maybe it's anchored.' She squinted. 'Funny, but there doesn't seem to be anybody on board.'

'It's a bit distant for a swim.' Aditya's tone was doubtful.

'We could use our boat.'

'That leaking tub! It will sink on us before we get there . . . but, yes, we could use it as far as it goes.'

'Shall we?' asked Chitra.

'Let's!' replied Aditya.

Chitra's heart beat faster. She half-skipped, half-ran to the boat. She hummed a tune as she helped Aditya push the leaking vessel to the water. Maybe their ordeal was finally coming to an end.

Aditya held the boat while Chitra collected the paddles and jumped in. Wading through the surf, he pushed the boat as far as he could, and when the swell wetted his chest, he pulled himself in. Though water was streaming in through the cracked hull, Aditya did not reach for the bailer. He grabbed one of the paddles from Chitra and together they powered the tiny boat forward.

White terns flapped above the beach as they pulled away. The sea eagles were still perched on their tree. Chitra was reminded of snowflakes when she looked at them—giant snowflakes. Thick jungle lined the shore on either side of the beach. The sun shone down upon the boat as they paddled out of the shadow of the trees. The sea was calm, with barely the hint of a swell, yet the boat steadily lost speed as they progressed. The reason was obvious; it was turning heavier as water flooded its hull.

'She's not going to make it,' declared Aditya.

Chitra nodded. 'We'll have to swim the last bit.'

Aditya paddled furiously. 'What is the boat doing there? It's certainly anchored.'

'There's still no one on board,' said Chitra, staring across the water.

'There's a cabin beneath the mast. There could be someone inside. But why would they anchor here, off the Jarawa coast?'

'Maybe cruising—' Chitra broke off. 'Look!' she exclaimed, pointing north.

Another boat was visible; not a fancy yacht like the one ahead. Although a long distance away, they could make out it was a country craft, probably a dungi.

'Phew!' Chitra exhaled loudly. 'Lots of traffic here on these waters. Rescue seems certain now.'

'I don't know,' said Aditya uncertainly. 'What if that is one of Patrick's boats?'

Chitra fell silent, and Aditya noticed that she had begun to row harder. Aditya bent his back too. The two of them rowed together, matching each other stroke for stroke. But despite their energetic paddling, their boat continued to lose speed, turning more sluggish with each passing minute.

'We are wasting our time,' said Chitra at last. 'We should swim if we want to make it to the yacht before the dungi arrives.'

Aditya wiped sweat from his eyes. The sea was calm and there wasn't a breath of wind. The country craft, though still far away, had altered its bearing and was now headed directly for them. The white yacht wasn't far. He looked down at the water in their boat. Its weight had dragged their vessel down. Their bow was riding inches above the sea, and swells were beginning to sweep across it, bringing in additional buckets of water.

'Right,' said Aditya, dropping his paddle. 'Let's swim.'

Chitra abandoned the boat first, diving over its side. Aditya followed, striking out behind her. The water was cool, and salt stung their eyes. Kicking hard, they broke into a rapid crawl.

DOWN UNDER

Bobbing and swaying, the white mast of the yacht guided them, in the manner a lighthouse might have. Aditya swam as fast as he could, but Chitra, much to his chagrin, drew steadily ahead. Chitra was working her arms as if the swim was a hundred-metre dash. Not only was she a strong swimmer, but at this moment—in addition to her natural abilities—her speed was fuelled by the heart-stopping possibility that Aditya's guess could be true.

Chitra ignored the pain that began to numb her chest and shoulders. Paying no heed to the heaviness growing in her arms, she concentrated on rhythm: one, two, breathe; one, two, breathe . . . But her breathing was not always smooth. Every once in a while a wave would slap her face just as she raised her gasping mouth, flooding it with water. She gagged often, swallowing and spitting seawater.

Presently, the deep blue of the water began to change, turning turquoise and then a light green. Sunlight rippled against the rising seabed, and in the haze Chitra spotted

coral and a quivering white rope—the boat was anchored above a reef. There were fish below, a shoal of large fish with funny, bumped heads.

The shadowed hull of the boat drew closer, and when Chitra passed the anchor rope she halted, raising her head. She breathed heavily as the boat rocked before her. Its hull was smooth and white, and a silver railing, bright in the morning light, encircled its deck. Its mast poked skywards from the roof of a low-slung cabin with small windows. The door of the cabin was open, and Chitra heard music. Strains of violins and flutes mingled with the hiss and slap of the sea.

There was no one on deck.

Kicking hard, Chitra swam around the boat, searching for a way up. There was a ladder on the port side. 'Hullo?' she shouted, pulling herself towards it. There had to be somebody on board; the music indicated so. Aditya had arrived beside her, and together they shouted once more.

'They can't hear us,' panted Aditya. 'Music's too loud. Let's climb on board.'

Chitra grabbed the ladder and dragged herself up. Dripping water, she rolled on to the deck.

'Good morning,' spoke a voice conversationally above her.

Chitra whipped her head around. Standing above her was a fair-skinned man of average height. He had long red hair combed backwards and tied in a ponytail. All he wore was a pair of shorts and rubber slippers. Aditya had pulled himself on board too, and the man was looking down at them, a quizzical expression on his face.

'Morning,' replied Chitra, rising to her feet. Suddenly conscious of her looks, she brushed her hair back behind her ears.

'Hi,' greeted Aditya, smiling and rising too.

Nodding, the red-haired man stared at them. 'Um,' he began uncertainly. 'Um . . . may I enquire what you are doing here?' His eyes were grey and the accent definitely British.

It was to Aditya that the question was addressed, and Chitra, nervous about the approaching dungi, turned her head. Her breath froze. The dungi was headed straight for the yacht.

'Sorry to barge in—' began Aditya, but he didn't finish because Chitra cut him off.

'We are on the run,' she spluttered. 'Men who want to kill us are chasing us.'

'*Kill you?*' queried the man, a dubious expression on his face.

'We've been on the run for two days,' continued Chitra. 'And even now . . . that boat—' she pointed behind her.

'It is Patrick,' said Aditya heavily, looking back across the blue sea.

'How can you tell?' asked Chitra, not wanting to believe him. 'The boat's too far, I can't recognise anyone.'

'I can see its green markings. Take cover, if he has binocs he will see us.' Moving swiftly, he stepped behind the cabin and ducked.

Chitra dashed after Aditya and squatted beside him.

Music blared from the cabin, reaching a crescendo. Everything seemed unreal to Chitra. She was sitting on the deck of a beautiful boat listening to loud rousing music—

yet, instead of elation at the turn of events, a terrible fear was building inside her.

The Englishman followed them. 'I'm sorry,' he said, 'I don't understand what's going on.'

Chitra paid no heed to the man. 'Can we make it back to the shore before they arrive?' she asked Aditya.

'No.' Aditya shook his head. 'Not a chance, they'll intercept us. That boat,' he continued, speaking to the Englishman. 'The men in it have guns. They are coming for us. Is there any place we can hide?'

'*Hide?*' asked the Englishman. He was shorter than both Chitra and Aditya, and the sun had turned his fair skin a light bronze. 'Where can you hide on this boat?'

'What do we do?' asked Chitra, despair writ large on her face.

Aditya didn't reply. There was nothing he could say.

'Excuse me,' spoke the Englishman. 'Are your lives really in danger?'

Chitra nodded dully.

'Have you dived before?' he asked.

'What?' asked Aditya, looking up.

'There is only one place to hide and that's underwater. I have scuba sets ready. You could dive and remain underwater while the boat is in the vicinity. My clients are below—that's why I'm here. You could join them. That's if you've been down before and know how to dive.'

'*I do!*' exclaimed Chitra and Aditya together.

'Are you sure?' asked the Englishman, looking closely at them. 'Be truthful. A single mistake and you can die underwater.'

'I've dived often in these waters,' claimed Chitra excitedly.

'And I've dived in Lakshadweep,' asserted Aditya.

The Englishman stared intently at the teenagers, assessing them. 'Okay,' he said finally. His voice turned businesslike. 'Wait here, I'll get the gear.' Turning, he strode to the cabin.

He returned almost immediately, lugging buoyancy vests with tanks strapped to them. 'The tanks are full. They should last up to an hour but estimate only forty-five minutes. Belt them on, I'll get the masks and flippers.'

The strains of the 'Blue Danube' floated from the cabin, and despite the imminent threat of Patrick and his boat, Chitra found herself humming along with the music as she strapped on her gear. The thrilling prospect of diving into a coral reef had transformed her mood. There was a buzz in her head, as if she was intoxicated, and, despite her efforts at controlling her excitement, her lips kept crinkling into a smile. Catching her eye, Aditya winked. There was a big grin on his face.

The boat tilted and Chitra turned her head.

A face, half-veiled behind a mask, was staring at her from the ladder. It was a delicate female face with wet, black, shoulder-length hair. The mask was pulled back and dark eyes stared at her in astonishment.

'Who on earth are you two?' expostulated an angry, high-pitched voice. 'What cheek! How dare you use my equipment without permission? Take it off—right now!'

'Cool down, Manavi,' called the Englishman from the cabin door. He stepped out with goggles and flippers in his hands. 'These kids seem to be in some kind of jam. A dungi is approaching. You can see it if you turn your head.'

'So?' said the lady, climbing on board. Behind her, Chitra and Aditya saw another head bobbing in the water.

'They say that there are men with guns on board the boat,' continued the Englishman. 'They are on the run from those men. The only place they can hide is underwater, so I'm sending them down.'

'*You are sending them down?*' asked Manavi, unbuckling her weight belt. 'You are sending them down?' she repeated, in a silken, disbelieving tone. Manavi was short and petite, and her skin was tanned a deep brown. Her face looked familiar; Chitra was sure she had seen her before. 'Have you asked them if they've dived before—whether they know how to use the equipment?'

Chitra and Aditya loudly reaffirmed their diving prowess.

'I promise we know how to dive,' added Chitra earnestly. 'We'll explain later. There is no time now. We have to hide from these men. If they see us, they might kill us.'

Manavi stared wordlessly, dripping streams of water. The diver behind her, heavy with scuba gear, pulled himself on board. The Englishman crossed over, handing Chitra and Aditya a set of masks and flippers each. Chitra recollected where she had seen Manavi. It was at Port Blair. Although she had never personally met her, she was aware that Manavi operated a scuba centre. She saw Manavi draw a breath and stride over to Aditya. Grabbing loose straps dangling from his vest, she tightened them.

'Check your air,' she instructed, handing him the mouthpiece. 'You too,' she ordered Chitra. 'Ben,' she called out to the Englishman, 'you've forgotten their weight belts.' The diver who had boarded behind Manavi was fair-skinned and blond-haired. He appeared lost as he watched the confusion on the deck.

Ben, the Englishman, returned with the belts. 'Quick,' he urged, as he handed them out. 'There isn't much time.'

Manavi flicked her eyes over the teenagers as they clipped on their belts. Aditya was ready first, and making sure that the cabin shielded him from the approaching dungi, Manavi led him to the nose of the boat. When Aditya had seated himself at the edge of the railing, she cupped her fingers in the 'okay' sign and nodded.

Clamping the mouthpiece between his teeth, Aditya jumped feet first into the water. Waddling awkwardly in her flippers, Chitra followed, and repeating Aditya's inelegant manoeuvre, she splashed in beside him.

The fins felt far more comfortable in the water as Chitra treaded the sea. Floating beside Aditya, she removed her mouthpiece and shouted, 'Follow me!'

'Okay,' came the muffled reply.

Chitra looked up. Ben was gesturing downwards with his hands, an urgent expression on his face. She caught the words, 'down . . . quick!' The rest were lost on her as she submerged herself.

The sounds of the ocean took over as the waters of the Andaman Sea closed above her. Having dived often, Chitra was familiar with the muted roar that soaked up all surface sounds. But this time, woven with the voices of the sea was the steady thump of a motor.

Seized by an intense desire to descend as rapidly as she possibly could, Chitra grabbed Aditya's hand, and kicking strongly, plunged to the seabed at a steep angle.

Meanwhile, on board, Manavi was preparing to enter the water again.

'Not changing your air tank?' enquired Ben.

'There's no need,' replied Manavi, clipping on her weight belt. 'I haven't used much. I returned only to bring Ryan back, he wasn't feeling good. The others are still down there—waiting for me.'

'You'll have to hide the kids. Visibility is pretty good; I can see the bottom clearly from here.'

'The boat's definitely heading this way, Ben,' said Manavi, as she sat on the railing. The dungi was just a few hundred metres away. 'Keep them occupied. There is a coral cave . . . buy me time to get them into the cave. Goodbye—I'm off.' Clutching her mask to her face, Manavi stepped into the sea.

From the seabed Chitra saw Manavi enter the water. In the distance, the long hull of the approaching dungi was visible. There were fish everywhere about her. A wondrous world surrounded her, but at this moment she had no eyes for it. Aditya, however, was thoroughly enraptured. She saw him floating over a brightly coloured clam whose thick, purple lips were embedded in a rock. The wavy lips snapped shut when Aditya ran his hands above them.

Chitra frowned. She stared at Aditya in exasperation as he searched the seabed for more clams. This was certainly not the time for frolic or diversions. She swam to Aditya and grabbed his arm. An expression of annoyance appeared behind his mask, but his face quickly sobered when she pointed to the surface. The dungi's long, narrow shadow was floating alongside the thicker shadow of the yacht.

Trailing a stream of bubbles, Manavi arrived beside them. Not halting, she motioned them to follow. She swam fast, skimming over sand and clumps of coral. Many hundred finger-sized fish hovered like a shimmering curtain to their left. Were they transparent, wondered Chitra, as she kicked hard, struggling to keep up with Manavi. The curtain quivered as Manavi swept past them. But for a yellow ring encircling their eyes, the fish were indeed transparent. Aditya stuck his hand out as he swam past. The curtain shivered, as if a wind had flapped it. For a brief moment it vanished and then re-materialised a few feet behind.

Sand stretched beneath them, patterned in tiny dunes. Soon they saw less sand as coral clumps began to appear, and it wasn't long before they were swimming over endless beds of intricate, dazzlingly coloured coral formations. Fish of all shapes and sizes darted everywhere, and Aditya, overcome by the watery world enveloping him, forgot once more about the danger lurking on the surface.

But Chitra hadn't and neither had Manavi. They both heard the change in pitch of the dungi's motor. Chitra glanced backwards and her body stiffened. The long shadow of the dungi was moving towards them. They were exposed on the coral and Chitra, experiencing the helplessness of a diver chased by a shark, searched desperately for a place to hide.

Manavi was pulling ahead, and Aditya was beginning to wander. If she could, Chitra would have screamed at her companion; but in the water, all she could do was tug violently at his arm and kick forward. Streams of bubbles drew Chitra's gaze as she swam frantically behind Manavi. Two divers were swimming towards Manavi. But though she had seen them, Manavi held her course, not deviating to meet them.

The coral dropped away ahead and Chitra saw Manavi swim downwards. An underwater valley appeared. A ledge fell away below Manavi, but a little ahead the seabed rose once more. Manavi was dropping into the area in-between.

Chitra almost lost her mouthpiece as she stared in open-mouthed fascination at the valley. Beautiful sea fans, thin and intricate, like delicate tapestry, hung on either side of the valley walls. Coloured in stunning shades of yellow and purple, the sea fans were like living curtains, stitched together by a divinely skilled tailor.

Pressure intensified in their ears as they followed Manavi, diving between the fans. The reverberations of the engine grew louder. They swallowed hard as they swam downwards, equalising continuously with the increasing water pressure.

Manavi had halted at the bottom. Floating above the sand she beckoned them. Chitra's heart leapt as she looked at the area behind Manavi. Thick coral formations projected like bizarre canopies from the slopes. There was a hollow underneath, like a cave. The umbrella-like coral would screen them from the surface. The sound of the motor grew ever louder as Chitra, followed closely by Aditya, shot into the coral cave. Panic welled in Chitra as the chugging boomed louder. Could they be seen from the surface? But her panic quelled when she turned her head upwards—nothing but coral was visible above her.

Thunderous reverberations suggested that the boat was directly above them. Signalling them to wait, Manavi swam out through the coral arch towards the approaching divers. Passing them, she kept going, swimming away from the coral cave. The divers turned and followed her. The reverberations above changed pitch, turning deeper—the dungi was moving. A shadow passed over the valley, advancing over the coral, pursuing Manavi and the divers.

Chitra held Aditya's arm as they watched Manavi and the divers swim away with the dungi trailing above. She reached out and hugged Aditya who responded by squeezing her in return. But in doing so they tangled wires and clinging to one another they laughed behind their masks.

There was sand at the bottom of the cave, and the leading edge of Aditya's flipper raked across it whilst he extricated his pipe from Chitra's. As Aditya raised his leg, a plume of sand shot upwards like an underwater explosion. The sand spread outwards, and as it settled, they saw what had caused the eruption. It was a fish—a lollipop-shaped fish, with a round head and a long tail. Chitra and Aditya instantly identified the fish.

A stingray!

The mist-like sand had camouflaged the creature, and Aditya's flipper had disturbed it while it lay resting.

Chitra and Aditya swiftly backed away. They were well aware that the long thin tail, jutting like a stick from the creature's head, had a nasty sting attached to it—a sting that could deliver a punch like an electric whip.

The stingray hovered above the cave floor, its round eyes staring at them. Its head was like a pancake, thought Chitra. As she watched, the folds of the pancake started to undulate, and the sting began to move. It swam slowly and gracefully from the cave, into the valley beyond, shedding sand that scattered like snow in the water. It pushed on at a leisurely pace, looking every bit like a flying saucer passing over an alien landscape.

The stingray was forgotten when a turtle appeared behind the valley wall. Chitra and Aditya spotted it simultaneously, and their eyes, abandoning the disappearing ray, locked on to the massive armoured denizen of the sea. Surprisingly, the humped creature wasn't ponderous; rather, it swam smoothly and elegantly, gliding effortlessly through the water. Chitra had seen several turtles in the Andaman waters, but today, after having held baby turtles in her hand, this sighting was special. Though the babies and the adults were identical in appearance—the head, the shell, the flippers were all the same—the disparity in their size was staggering. The scrabbling, palm-sized babies that the crabs and birds had plucked from the sand would have to feed for years to mature into the massive, confident creature passing before them.

Aditya transferred his attention to what lay below him after the turtle sailed past. Keen to avoid any further surprises, he carefully inspected the sand. He spotted several tiny fish on the powdery floor. One was behaving rather oddly, moving continuously up and down, as if satisfying an itch against the sand. At the far edge of the cave, he saw a cylindrical body, half-covered by sand. It was curled, looking like a discarded rubber pipe. It lay on the sea floor, utterly motionless, and Aditya, identifying it, wondered how the harmless creature had managed to elude the questing eyes of poachers. It was a sea cucumber—the defenceless marine animal that was sought by the intruders from Myanmar.

Beside the cucumber lay a starfish with several arms. It was coloured a bright purple, and like the cucumber, it too lay motionless in the sand.

Chitra was pulling his arm, pointing behind. Turning, Aditya saw a large fish staring at them. It was a grouper. The fish, almost stationary in the water, stared suspiciously at them through big, wary eyes.

Trailing bubbles, Chitra and Aditya floated under the protective cover of the coral umbrella. The varied designs of the coral formations surrounding them were strange and bizarre—otherworldly, thought Chitra, as she gazed at them. The simplest of the formations looked like rocks—textured rocks in different shades of brown, yellow and gold. Then there were those that jutted horizontally from the slope, utterly flat, like tabletops. Some, resting on the seabed, were almost perfectly round, like giant marbles, and had an elaborate pattern etched on them. There were those that looked like prickly cactus bushes and others that resembled exquisite rugs draped on undersea mountain walls.

The coral was like a living forest, and what added to its extraterrestrial feeling were the colours. Every possible hue and shade of the spectrum was displayed. Gaudy purples, flashy greens, sizzling reds, dull yellows, mushroom browns and peacock blues—it was as if a child with a distinct preference for the loud and garish had run amok with a paint brush.

The world around them was in motion. Fish were darting everywhere, and even the apparently motionless ones were being swayed by a gently pulsing current. Microscopic plankton and organic matter swirled like a fine mist. Chitra was aware that the tiny, almost indistinguishable plankton were the primary food source of the sea.

Ahead, perched atop spiky staghorn coral projections, Chitra spotted two plankton-feeding feather stars. She swam towards them holding Aditya's hand. About two feet long, they possessed several undulating arms that looked like exquisite marine feathers. Their feathery arms unfurled in the currents trapping the floating plankton.

So enthralling was the world around them that Chitra's nervousness lapsed, and the threat of Patrick and his boat faded. She and Aditya swam side by side, marvelling at the beauty and diversity of the creatures of a coral ecosystem.

Chitra felt Aditya tugging her. He was pointing to an area on the sea floor that was covered with what looked like purple hay.

Sea anemone!

The teenagers swam forward and hovered over a purple underwater bush. Chitra searched amidst the mop-like strands. Yes! Aditya saw them too. Two tiny clownfish, striped ochre and white, were peering fearfully at them from deep within the anemone. Chitra passed her hands over the anemone strands, and both fish dived deep inside, disappearing from view.

Chitra was aware that they had left the shelter of the coral cave, but it didn't matter since there was no sign of Patrick's boat. She followed Aditya as he swam towards a parrotfish that was pecking away at the knobby protrusions of a golden-brown, boulder-like coral formation. They could both distinctly hear the fish as its strong, beak-like jaws gnawed at the coral.

Spotting a couple of bright yellow fish, they swam towards them. The thin envelope-like fish with pointed snouts were Chitra's favourite reef dwellers. Butterfly fish. But it wasn't just their beautiful colours and shapes that attracted Chitra; she was charmed by the fact that she invariably saw them in lovey-dovey pairs. This pair was bright yellow with blue circles around their eyes, and they cast furtive glances at Aditya and Chitra as they followed them. Aditya accelerated forward, but when he came near, they darted into a coral crevice. Turning, they stared at him from the safety of their tiny cave.

Chitra saw Aditya hurriedly back away. Looking down, she spotted what had alarmed him, but instead of reversing like Aditya, she swam forward. Creeping on the sandy bed was a sea snake. About a metre long, its bright black and white bands were distinctive, as also its flat, paddle-shaped tail.

The snake, in a manner similar to snakes on land, was slithering along the sand. Though Chitra had no intention

of touching the sea-going reptile, her enthrallment at having spotted it drew her hypnotically forward.

But a sudden burst of bubbles and a sharp tug on her arm broke the spell. Chitra turned in annoyance and goggled when she saw Manavi beside her. There was a stern expression in Manavi's eyes, and she held Chitra in a firm grip. She shook her head, and holding on to Chitra, turned away from the snake. Chitra followed reluctantly, casting glances at the banded reptile that was now crawling into the coral.

Firmly holding Chitra's hand, Manavi led them back through the mesmerising sea fan section. The two divers they had spotted on the way to the cave were floating at the foot of the underwater valley. One was a fair-skinned lady with short blonde hair, and the other was a man with a darker, wheatish complexion.

Manavi halted beside the divers. Sunlight speared down from the blue above, and plankton sparkled in its dancing shafts. Manavi waited for them to settle and then swam around them, moving her hands over their equipment. Satisfied, she cupped her fingers at them. Both Aditya and Chitra responded positively. Nodding, Manavi turned and set off.

Fish moved out of their way. The thrill and excitement of their underwater escapade had purged all thoughts of Patrick and his dungi from both Chitra and Aditya's thoughts. Their eyes swept continuously from side to side, absorbing the beauty of the seascape about them. It was with disappointment that they saw the coral formations begin to scatter and sand appear between them. But there were several shoals of fish to distract them. They entered a group of large blue and yellow fish—fusiliers, Chitra was convinced—that disbanded above and below them. Later, a group of yellow-green, finger-sized fish with green lines quivered in a synchronised tango and skittered away from them. But from afar the fish appeared blue instead of green.

Ahead, they saw stalks of green on the sand. The carpet of green was seagrass, and its sword-like leaves undulated in the current. Chitra blinked. Floating above the seagrass was a large creature. Manavi had seen the creature too, and she had turned and was swimming towards it.

Chitra couldn't believe their luck.

They had spotted a dugong.

Manatee was another name for the creature. But 'sea cow', as the animal is also known, was more descriptive, in Chitra's opinion. Having been hunted almost to extinction, dugongs are now amongst the rarest creatures of the Andaman Sea. And unbelievably, floating right before her eyes, was one of the remnants of the decimated species.

The dugong floated above the grass, watching them approach. In size it was comparable to a seal, but in stroke and movement, it projected the grace of a floating rhinoceros. Its snout was wrinkled and rounded, its skin grey and folded. Chitra knew that it was a harmless animal. Dugongs are docile, unhurried browsers of the sea floor. Taking advantage of their docility, hunters spear them, killing them simply for sport. Speeding motorboats had also contributed to their decline, mowing down the slow-moving animals before they could move out of their path.

The dugong was turning. Manavi had halted, and the others circled beside her. Glancing back often, the slow-paced animal swam away from them, and Manavi reluctantly turned away.

The shadow of the yacht's hull was visible in the distance. They were still swimming under several feet of water, and Manavi rose gradually as they neared the yacht. A shoal of fish was swimming close to the surface, and Aditya pointed them out to Chitra. It was while they were watching the shoal that a sudden explosion of water and air took place amidst it. In quick succession, they saw the underside of a bird, its legs and a large beak. It was a white bird—a tern. Its head appeared for a brief instant, and in a flash its beak had seized a fish. It all happened in a twinkling: one moment the bird was there, and the next it was lifting off with a fish in its beak, and the rest of the shoal was diving down, one member short.

Chitra shot upwards, surfacing even before Manavi. Through her dripping mask she saw the tern winging above the water with a silvery fish grasped firmly in its beak. Turning, she spotted the boat and Ben, the Englishman, on its deck. The others were surfacing beside the boat, and spitting out her mouthpiece, Chitra swam towards them. Ben did not allow Chitra or Aditya to board.

'Wait!' he shouted down at them. 'The dungi hasn't gone away. They're watching us.' Chitra and Aditya floated obediently in the water while the others pulled themselves on board.

'They're refusing to go away,' Ben informed from the deck. 'They've halted halfway to the shore, beside a half-sunken boat. Is that yours?'

Chitra and Aditya exchanged worried looks. 'It is ours,' shouted Chitra, holding on to the ladder.

'Maybe we should get moving,' suggested Manavi, standing beside Ben.

'Right,' replied the ponytailed Englishman. He turned to Chitra and Aditya. 'Hang on there,' he instructed, 'they are watching us. Climb on board when the boat starts moving. Mind you, don't leave it till too late. You'll get swept away when I pick up speed.'

Ben disappeared inside the cabin, and the motor cranked with a purr. Water flowed past Chitra and Aditya as the yacht started forward. Chitra climbed up first and flattening herself, rolled on board. Aditya followed, and when he was safely on deck, Ben opened the throttle.

'It's all right,' said Manavi. 'Don't worry about them seeing you now, they won't be able to catch us. This boat's too fast for a dungi.'

'But they've got guns,' said Chitra, reaching to remove her flippers.

'Rifles?' asked Manavi.

'No, handguns,' answered Aditya, undoing his weight belt buckle.

'It should be okay,' said Manavi. 'I think we're out of range of handguns, but stay down for a couple of minutes in any case.'

The yacht cut through the water, bucking the swell. The diver who had stayed back on board was sitting on the deck next to the blonde-haired lady, helping her remove her gear. The man with the darker skin—an Indian, thought Chitra—was standing at the nose of the boat. Manavi had stalked off to the cabin, and she returned shortly with a pair of binoculars in her hands.

'Are those men poachers?' asked Manavi, squatting beside Chitra.

'We don't know,' replied Aditya, who like Chitra, was lying flat on the deck. 'They could be smugglers. We stumbled on to their camp, and they captured us. Our friends are still being held by them. Is there a radio on board?'

Manavi shook her head. 'Sorry, there isn't. Ben's communication equipment was giving him trouble. He is on a round-the-world voyage, but because of the breakdown he halted at Port Blair. I'm renting his boat while his radio's being repaired. The divers on board are my clients.

'I wouldn't worry about the radio if I were you—this boat is fast. We'll be at Wandoor Jetty in a matter of hours. You can call from there. I'll make the call if you like. I know the coastguard people well. The chief will despatch a helicopter in a matter of minutes once I tell him. Your friends will be rescued and flown to Port Blair before sundown. Stop worrying about them, or for yourselves, for that matter.'

Manavi smiled, and rising she looked aft, pressing the binoculars to her eyes.

'You can stand up,' she shouted, her wet hair blowing in the wind. 'We're far enough now.'

Having unfastened his gear while lying on deck, Aditya rose quickly to his feet. No match for the speeding yacht, the dungi had fallen way behind, well out of gunshot range. Manavi handed Aditya the binoculars. Viewing wasn't easy on the pitching deck, but from the glimpses he managed, he clearly recognised Patrick's heavy face. Patrick's body seemed to go rigid as Chitra rose and stood beside him.

Aditya raised his arm and waved.

Chitra laughed and waved too. 'Has he seen us?' she asked Aditya.

'He has . . . but he is a remarkably cool customer. There's no anger or despair on his face.'

'His boat's turning,' said Manavi.

Sure enough, the dungi was turning, setting a northerly course up the coast.

It didn't immediately strike either Chitra or Aditya that their ordeal was drawing to a close. Only as the two boats drew steadily apart did it begin to sink in that Patrick had abandoned the chase.

'Smile!' enthused Manavi. 'What is it with you kids? Can't you see that you've escaped? You're free!'

Aditya surprisingly reacted in a subdued manner. All he felt was a sense of relief.

But Chitra exulted.

Her feelings came pouring out in the form of a sudden unladylike yell of triumph. A tern, perched on the mast, squawked and flew away in alarm. The divers gazed at her.

But Chitra didn't care.

'*Yippee!*' she whooped, pumping her fists like a cheerleader, an expression of unbridled joy on her face.

Yes, it was over!

Those unending hours of despair and danger were behind them. They had outwitted and outlasted Patrick and his men. They would be at Port Blair in a matter of hours. Vikram and Alex's rescue was certain now. The coastguard would set them free by evening.

Chitra turned to Aditya, her voice dropping, hushed and disbelieving now.

'We made it,' she whispered, bringing her hands to her cheeks. 'We made it . . . Aditya . . . we made it!' Tears glistened in Chitra's eyes as she stared at her friend.

Her exuberance snapped Aditya from his reverie. Manavi and the divers watched as Aditya, laughing at Chitra, raised his hand. The girl reached up, and the two friends exchanged a resounding high-five.

ANDAMAN NEWS CLIPS

FROM *ANDAMAN ADVENTURE—BARREN ISLAND*

*** *Chapter 1* ***

Helicopter Rescue

Vikram Singh, a teenaged tourist and his Karen boatman were dramatically rescued by helicopter from a secret hideout in Jarawa territory this evening.

Two friends of the rescued tourist—Chitra Shankaran and Aditya Khan—had escaped earlier from the same hideout. Evading their captors, they reached Port Blair by boat this afternoon and alerted the authorities.

According to a naval spokesman, a helicopter was despatched immediately, and the young tourist and the Karen boatman were liberated before darkness fell. Their captors, however, had disappeared without a trace. Refusing to divulge further details the spokesman said that the Commander-in-Chief of the islands, Admiral Bijoy Prakash, would throw light on the investigations at a press conference scheduled for tomorrow.

Extract from the **Andaman Times**, *Monday, 7 January.*

Arms Smuggling in the Islands?

The shadow of gun-running looms once more over the Bay Islands.

Though he did not deny the possibility, Admiral Bijoy Prakash refused to confirm that the youngsters who escaped from captivity in the Jarawa forests had stumbled upon an arms smuggling operation. 'Nothing was found at the hideout,' was the admiral's response, when questioned. 'The camp had been cleared by the time our people arrived,' he explained. 'A large godown and crane facilities indicate that heavy material had been stored there. I am not denying that it could be for arms and weaponry. But it could also be for storing wood from the forests; it could be anything of value.'

Mr Ramesh, Chief of Intelligence, who was also present, said that the teenagers involved could not attend the press conference since they were tired and were resting. Two of the teenagers, Vikram Singh and Aditya Khan, were schoolboys who were visiting the islands on holiday. The third, Ms Chitra Shankaran, was the daughter of ornithologist and researcher, Dr Ravi Shankaran. They had been travelling

• • • • • •

to Interview Island by dungi before they detoured down a creek to search for crocodiles.

When questioned, Mr Ramesh acknowledged that the creek they had ventured down lay in Jarawa territory and that entering it was illegal. But he also clarified that Ms Chitra Shankaran, in her capacity as a member of the island reptile research group, had prior security clearance to enter the creek. It was at the far end of the creek that they had discovered the hideout and had been captured.

Mr Ramesh added that the underground network the teenagers had uncovered was large, well-financed and well-organised. Though only guesswork at this moment, it was highly likely that it had been in operation for some time. Mr Ramesh admitted that failure to detect its existence earlier was a security lapse.

The Commander-in-Chief announced that the highest priority had been attached to this matter and that investigations were being conducted on a war footing. Since the affair fell under the purview of the Intelligence Department, Mr Ramesh would be heading the investigation, and resources from the coastguard, navy and police would be made available to him.

Mr Ramesh said that leads had already been established and were being investigated. The recuperating youngsters would throw further light on the matter when they were debriefed. Due to security compulsions, details and progress of the investigation would not be revealed on a day-to-day basis. The press would be informed when notable developments or breakthroughs occurred.

A detailed report on arms smuggling and the utility of the Andaman Islands as a staging site will appear in our Sunday Edition.

Extract from the **Andaman Times**, *Tuesday, 8 January.*

• • • • • •

Don't miss the exciting conclusion to
Andaman Adventure: The Jarawa*!*

Read more from the next book
in the series.

Andaman Adventure: Barren Island

Vikram, Aditya and Chitra—recuperating from their adventures in the Jarawa jungles —are at Port Blair, the capital city of the Andaman Islands. Stumbling on a series of intriguing clues, Vikram pursues them, tracking the men who had abducted him earlier. But powerful criminals thwart his endeavours and, unable to escape their wrath, Vikram is forced to undertake a voyage destined for unknown shores.

In a remote corner of the Andaman Sea lies an island called Barren. On this uninhabited and forgotten outpost of India, Vikram discovers that it is not just a band of desperate men that he must pit his wits against. Primal forces of nature, the very ones that shaped our planet, are at work on Barren, and the smouldering narrative comes to a fiery climax on the island's lonely shores.

Journey to the Andamans in the concluding instalment of this riveting tale of adventure and mystery, set in India's far-flung islands.

EPILOGUE

Where did the original black inhabitants of the Andaman Islands come from? It is a mystery that has puzzled scientists and anthropologists across the world. Today, every corner of our planet has been settled by our human species. In most cases, historical clues and evidence, like the existence of similar races, help researchers establish ancient migration routes and trace the origin of the different peoples of our world. Anthropologists can determine the migration of American Indians to the continent of America; and the lineage of the Aryans and Dravidians. But clues to the ancestry of the black Andaman race are difficult to come by. It isn't easy to rationally explain how an isolated band of black people arrived in this remote corner of Asia.

Lieutenant Blair, who first surveyed the Andaman Islands, was of the opinion that the Andamanese are the descendants of black African slaves. According to him and other British administrators of that time, these African slaves were on board a Portuguese slave ship that ran aground on the islands. Historical records of maritime explorations reveal that the Portuguese arrived in the waters of the Indian Ocean only in the fifteenth century. So, if we assume that Lieutenant Blair's theory is true, then the Andamanese have been around in the islands for only six hundred years.

But the fact that a black race has occupied the islands for millennia is established beyond doubt. Accounts of their existence have been recorded by travellers and seafarers from the second century onwards. Marco Polo passed by the islands in 1290 AD and penned an unflattering report, referring to the Andamanese as cannibals (which they are not). The people of Malaysia have known of the islands since ancient times, and they referred to its black inhabitants as the 'Handumans'. Handuman was the way the Malays pronounced Hanuman. The Malays were aware of the story of Lord Rama, and they believed that the black race of the Andamans were the descendants of Hanuman. Though there is no real proof, several historians maintain that the name Andaman is derived from the word 'Handuman' and that it was the epic Ramayana that gave the islands their name.

The Andaman Islands lie in the Bay of Bengal. The closest landfall from the islands is Myanmar, at 600 kilometres. The Indian ports of Chennai and Kolkata are 1200 kilometres away. The archipelago's neighbouring countries are Malaysia and Thailand. It is obvious that the Andamanese, when they migrated to the islands, must have done so from the shores of one or more of these countries. But the majority of the peoples of these countries bear no resemblance whatsoever to the inhabitants of the Andaman Islands. So then where did the Andamanese come from?

The theory that holds today explains that the Andamanese are of Negrito stock. Negrito is not to be mistaken with the African Negro. Though both races are dark skinned, their body proportions are entirely different. While the African Negro is tall, the Negrito is small; in fact, Negritos are amongst the smallest people in the world.

It is believed that many thousands of years ago the Andaman Islands were connected to the coast of Myanmar by a land bridge. At that time Myanmar and its neighbouring areas were populated by a black Negrito people. These Negritos were a simple people who hadn't yet discovered agriculture. They gathered edible crops and fruits, and they hunted game in the forest. People who do not subsist on agriculture and who, instead, hunt and gather, are called hunter-gatherers. The Negritos were all hunter-gatherers.

During the period that the land bridge existed, a section of the Negrito population crossed over to the islands. This migration continued for years, and the Negritos settled the islands. Their spread and distribution, however, was limited to the Andamans. They never made it to the Nicobar Islands, even though just a few hundred kilometres separate the island chains. Obviously, no land bridge existed between the Andamans and the Nicobars and the inability of the black race to cross over is testimony to their seafaring incompetence. The years passed, maybe centuries, maybe millennia, and geological changes began to occur. Subsidence took place, and the land bridge disappeared under the sea, cutting off the Andaman Islands from the mainland.

In the years that followed, the Negritos of the mainland disappeared. No one is sure how, but it is conjectured that other races (probably more advanced than the Negritos), swept across Myanmar, completely annihilating them. Though their ancestors were wiped out, the Negritos who had migrated to the Andaman Islands survived. The surrounding sea and the isolation of their islands preserved the Andamanese, allowing their race to endure till modern times. Isolation, however, is a double-edged sword. Whilst races on the mainland, through contact with other cultures and populations, absorbed fresh ideas and advanced technologically, the Andamanese remained as they were. When the British decided to establish a penal colony in the islands in 1858, the Andamanese were still leading hunter-gatherer lives, virtually unchanged from their existence when their ancestors crossed over thousands of years ago.

During their initial years on the islands, the British believed that the short black natives who stoutly resisted their attempts to settle were all one people. Though they were all Negritos, the Andamanese had by then evolved into several distinct tribes. There were twelve tribes who roamed the islands at that time. The British, for the sake of simplicity, clubbed ten of these tribes together and called them the Great Andamanese. Since it was their land that the British originally settled, it was the Great Andamanese that they befriended first. The Onge, the tribe that occupied Little Andaman Island, were befriended later. But the Jarawa and the Sentinelese (an offshoot of the Jarawa), resisted all overtures by the British and remained implacably hostile to them and to the Indian Administration that followed.

It is estimated that the combined population of the tribes of the Andamans was about 6000 when the British arrived. Of these the majority were the Great Andamanese. Today, however, the Great Andamanese have almost been wiped out, while the Jarawa, Sentinelese and the Onge survive (though all in small numbers).

Having lived isolated on their islands for thousands of years, the Negrito people of the Andamans had never been exposed to the diseases of the mainland. Catastrophically for them, the British administrators and the Indian 'convicts' who came to the islands brought with them the ills of the mainland, carrying diseases like chickenpox, measles, ophthalmia and syphilis. The Great Andamanese, because of their friendship with the British, were exposed to these diseases; and lacking the necessary resistance, it wasn't long before epidemics broke out amongst them.

It wasn't just diseases that destroyed the Great Andamanese. British-enforced disruption of their lives contributed equally. In the typical manner of the colonialists of that era, the British attempted to 'civilise' the natives. They urged them to live in houses, made them wear clothes and taught them to eat rice—none of which were natural to the forest-dwelling Andamanese. In addition (and inevitably so), the Andamanese discovered the vices of tobacco and alcohol from their masters and became addicted to them.

To begin with, the Great Andamanese were robust and strong, and their population held. But it wasn't long before their race was broken, and they became disease-ridden. Within fifty years of the occupation of their forests they began to die like flies. Even though they eventually acquired immunity to the diseases that ravaged them, they never overcame the despair of the loss of their simple jungle lives. Overwhelmed by us and our 'civilised' ways, the Great Andamanese lost the will to live. The Great Andamanese are now virtually extinct. Only forty individuals remain, and even today, their remnants are struggling to cope with vices and our 'civilisation' that we have forced on them.

It was the unrelenting defiance of the Jarawa that saved them from the horrible fate of the Great Andamanese. The Jarawa stoutly resisted all attempts by the British to befriend them and thereby avoided the diseases that afflicted the Great Andamanese. Never afraid to use their bows and arrows they attacked intruders who entered their territory. Their unceasing hostility denied the British the opportunity to teach them how to wear clothes or live in houses or eat their kind of food. They persisted instead with their simple 'uncivilised' lives and remained strong, healthy and purposeful.

It wasn't just the British that the Jarawa resisted. The Japanese, who briefly ruled the islands during the Second World War, couldn't tame them either. Even after independence and the advent of Indian rule their defiance did not waver. They fiercely protected their land and their way of life, not hesitating to kill when necessary. Fed up with their unrelenting belligerence, the Indian Government adopted fresh measures and attempted to befriend the Jarawa instead. They sent out friendship parties to Jarawa beaches and stacked gifts of food, tools and implements on their shores. There is no doubt that some headway was achieved in befriending the Jarawa. But their ingrained distrust for outsiders did not waver, and they rejected outright attempts to persuade them to abandon their hunter–gatherer lifestyle.

In the past few decades, the population of the Andaman Islands has been steadily rising. In their search for land, settlers have staked out farms, destroyed forests and encroached areas reserved for the Jarawa. The Jarawa responded in their traditional manner, and even though their weapons were limited to spears and arrows, the settlers quickly learned to fear and respect them.

But an additional problem, far deadlier than encroaching settlers, was brewing for the Jarawa. The Island Administration had been toying for years with the idea of building a road that would connect Port Blair with the northern ports of Mayabunder and Diglipur. No overland connection existed between the northern and southern sections of the islands, and the local population had been pressing the Administration for a permanent road. The Administration had held back because such a road would have to pass through the very heart of the Jarawa forests. Though environmentalists and anthropologists warned them of catastrophic consequences for the Jarawa if they went ahead, the Administration eventually caved in, flagging a green signal.

The construction of the Andaman Trunk Road took several years. The Jarawa bitterly resented this intrusion in their forests. Violence has been their traditional fallback for ensuring the undisturbed enjoyment of their way of life and the Jarawa displayed their anger by continuously attacking and raiding construction camps. But the Administration pushed on regardless, and the Trunk Road became a reality.

No sooner was it completed than buses and cars began to stream through the Jarawa forests. Though traffic is regulated, the road disrupted the secluded harmony of their lives. It wasn't long before Jarawa women and children, out of curiosity, began to appear on the road. Suddenly, the dreaded Jarawa were visible. Local people and officials rushed to see them, and enterprising businessmen started operating Jarawa tours.

Not long after the Andaman Trunk Road became operational the Island Administration received its first jolt. An epidemic of measles struck down almost half the Jarawa population. Though timely intervention and medicines saved the Jarawa, a warning bell was sounded. The Jarawa were no different from their late cousins, the Great Andamanese. The Jarawa too had no resistance to our diseases.

Will the Jarawa face the same fate as the Great Andamanese? There are a growing number of people who believe that unless the Andaman Trunk Road is shut down and several other measures taken, the Jarawa will quickly die out. But like any debate of far-reaching consequences, there are two sides to the argument. While there are those who advocate that the Jarawa should be left as they are, there exists another section of people who believe that the Jarawa must change and become like us. By withholding education from them we are committing a crime, they say. We are denying the Jarawa the right to wear clothes and enjoy modern conveniences. The Jarawa are Indian citizens like you and me. The policy of leaving them alone condemns their race to a primeval existence with no hope of advancing their lives. Should we as a modern nation willingly allow such a fate to overtake our countrymen?

The environmentalists argue that earlier attempts to 'civilise' the Great Andamanese had disastrous results. Has anyone asked the Jarawa whether they want to abandon their hunter-gatherer lives? Is it the Jarawa who have requested us to 'civilise' them? Have they expressed the desire to clone our ways? Have we forgotten the hopeless despair of the Great Andamanese? Can't we see the evidence before our eyes? Do not repeat past mistakes, warn the environmentalists. The Great Andamanese died out on account of disease and despair. The Jarawa are happy and healthy. LEAVE THEM ALONE!

Not far from the Jarawa reserves live a forgotten people called the Sentinelese. Though their island is only a few hours journey from Port Blair they are as yet unaffected by the crisis that threatens the survival of their brothers, the Jarawa. Surrounded by the sea, they live in splendid isolation. To this day they lead comfortable and unhurried lives. Though their existence is primitive they express no desire to change this state of affairs. Their unstinting hostility to landing parties demonstrates their commitment to protecting their simple ways.

Today, North Sentinel Island is the most amazing human time capsule on earth. Nowhere on our planet will you find such a pure, untouched race. The Jarawa together with the Sentinelese are a human treasure—a treasure we cannot afford to lose. That they will eventually be absorbed into our mainstream civilisation is inevitable. But change should not be forced on them. Change, if requested by them, should be at their pace and sensitive to their requirements. We should not forget that the entire Andaman Archipelago once belonged to them. Though they will never be masters of the islands again, it is our duty to at least allow them to be masters of their destiny.

READ MORE IN THE SERIES

Lakshadweep Adventure

Far out in the Arabian Sea, where the waters plunge many thousands of metres to the ocean floor, lies a chain of bewitching coral atolls—the Lakshadweep Islands. Vikram and Aditya dive into lagoons with crystal-clear water and reefs that are deep and shrouded in mystery. But when they stumble upon a devious kidnapping plot, their idyllic holiday turns into a desperate struggle for survival.

Forced out into the sea in the eye of a raging storm, they endure a shipwreck, only to be marooned on a remote coral island.

Journey through these breathtaking islands with a tale of scuba diving and sabotage, set in one of India's most splendid destinations.

READ MORE IN THE SERIES

Ranthambore Adventure

THIS IS THE STORY OF A TIGER

Once a helpless ball of fur, Genghis emerges as a mighty predator, the king of the forest. But the jungle isn't just his kingdom. Soon, Genghis finds himself fighting for his skin against equally powerful predators but of a different kind—humans.

The very same ones that Vikram and Aditya get embroiled with when they attempt to lay their hands on a diary that belongs to a ruthless tiger poacher. Worlds collide when an ill-fated encounter plunges the boys and their friend Aarti into a thrilling chase that takes them deep into the magnificent game park of Ranthambore.

Journey through the wilderness, brimming with tiger lore, with a tale set in one of India's most splendid destinations.

READ MORE IN THE SERIES

Ladakh Adventure

On their visit to the Changthang plateau of Ladakh, Vikram and Aditya find themselves on the run along with Tsering, a young Tibetan boy they meet while camping on this grand yet barren frontier of India. Determined to protect Tsering from the mysterious band of men chasing him, the three boys traverse the majestic land beyond the Himalayas in search of answers.

Who is Tsering? Why is he being hunted with such fierce resolve? Follow Vikram and Aditya across the remote frozen plateau to the mountain city of Leh—through a land of startling contrasts and magnificent mountains—as a perilous game of hide-and-seek unfolds.

Journey to the roof of the world with an enthralling tale set in one of India's most splendid destinations.

READ MORE IN THE SERIES

Snow Leopard Adventure

Vikram and Aditya are back in magnificent Ladakh. Having finally freed their young friend Tsering from the hands of dangerous men, they've set themselves up for an even greater challenge: to track down the grey ghost of the Himalayas, the snow leopard. The boys join a team of ecologists and explorers in their search for this rare and beautiful creature.

Here, Vikram befriends a troubled and unhappy girl called Caroline. The soaring peaks of the Himalayas hold no attraction for her, yet she is driven by an overpowering desire to spot a snow leopard. Set amidst majestic mountains and plunging valleys, *Snow Leopard Adventure* is a satisfying finale to a chase that began in *Ladakh Adventure*.

Journey in search of the elusive snow leopard with an enthralling tale set in one of India's most splendid destinations.

READ MORE IN THE SERIES

Sahyadri Adventure: Anirudh's Dream

Once upon a time, there were fields in the city of Mumbai. In its heartland were forests where panthers roamed. In those days, the seas flooded the channels that separated the seven islands of the city. On one of those islands was a fort guarded by cannons that bristled from black ramparts.

Vikram had no idea of the existence of this fort. Nor did his friend, Anirudh. But in a cave, on a windswept Sahyadri mountain, Anirudh had a dream. He dreamt of a boy named Irfan who once lived in this fort.

Journey to the Sahyadris in the first part of this riveting tale where history meets adventure in one of the most beautiful locales of India.

READ MORE IN THE SERIES

Sahyadri Adventure: Koleshwar's Secret

Searching for the remnants of Mumbai's fort is a futile exercise, for not a wall or battlement of the edifice survives today. But waking from his dream, Anirudh inexplicably knows every gate, contour and detail of the vanished fort. Fascinated by Anirudh's revelations, Vikram explores Mumbai with him.

Far out in the Sahyadri rises a mountain known as Koleshwar. Striving to make sense of his dream, Anirudh stumbles upon a forgotten legacy that leads to the mountain. Buried on its ancient slopes is a secret that only he has the power to decode.

Journey to the Sahyadris in the concluding instalment of this riveting tale where history meets adventure in one of the most beautiful locales of India.